Surrey Hills SuperHeroes

Steve Markwell

Cathy Coleman

To. Willow and Rowan

From Steve Ize
Anthn

From Steve the author.

The stories in this book are dedicated to the people who live and work in the Surrey Hills. They enjoy the privilege of life in an area of Outstanding Natural Beauty. They carry the responsibility of keeping the area beautiful, and sustaining the natural environment. Like many others on the planet, they struggle with balancing work, the desire to attract others into the area so they too may enjoy, and sustaining all that is good about the place they live. The stories in the book all deal with characters, real and imaginary, who have struggled in a similar way.

There are many I want to thank for supporting this book: Sophie Best at Silent Pool Distillery for giving me the SuperHero idea; the founders and staff at the Distillery who helped me understand the power of story and legend; Rob Fairbanks at the Surrey Hills AONB Organisation who supported the writing of the stories; Wendy Varcoe and her team at the Surrey Hills Enterprise Group who encouraged me to tell stories at events and festivals they have organised; Claire and Gemma, who are Enterprise members, both of whom appear in the book.

Thanks to Mark and Marianne, who along with Gemma, allowed me to publish their "Real life SuperHero" stories.

I also want to thank: my three children, Candace, Georgia and John, all of whom have faithfully read my stories, and provided honest input; my six grandchildren; Dylan, Amy, Cam, Matt, Fred and Eben who all listened to the stories without complaint (Amy and Matt appear in the stories. Cam, Matt and Fred all provided great input how the illustrations should look); I thank my sister Gloria, for encouragement and critique through the process.

Thanks to Stefan and Marcus's team at Vantage Publishing for providing on–going expertise and advice on the publication of the book.

Most of all, thanks to my mega talented wife, Liz, who tolerated, supported, inspired, proof read and edited throughout the process.

From Cathy the Illustrator.

Thank you to Mikey and my parents for always being so supportive and encouraging me to do what I love.

Published in 2022 by Vantage Publishing Limited
9 Chestnut Suite, Guardian House, Godalming, Surrey GU7 2AE

www.vantagepublishing.co.uk

ISBN: 978-1-8383469-5-9

Contents: -

PROLOGUE FOR ADULTS OF ALL AGES.

In the end, everything is magic.

Think about the vastness of the universe. The stars. The Sun, the great giver of life. The Moon, waxing and waning. The planets, meteors and asteroids. Now joined by the shimmering paths of satellites and aeroplanes.

Our Blue Planet, beautiful in its own right. Host and home to millions of living things. Trees, plants, fungi, insects, animals, fish, molluscs, amphibians, mammals, birds. From microscopic to gigantic. All colours, all different ways of breathing, eating, drinking, moving, living, reproducing. All endlessly impacting and relating to other living things in infinitely different ways.

Our Blue Planet. Thousand upon thousands of different landscapes; vast oceans, fresh water, frozen tundra. Always changing; everyday, something different, something new. Warmer, colder, windier, calmer. Friendlier, more dangerous, predictably consistent, suddenly dramatically unexpected.

Let's talk about the magic of words and pictures. We humans have a skill important beyond all others. We relate the magic of what we experience generation to generation. We call it storytelling, we call it legends, myths, fables, reporting, recording, showing. We call it history. We call it art. We call it media, theatre and dance. We call it education. All ways of telling others the magic we experience.

Let's move the focus from our universe and our planet, and think about our small group of islands.

Our image of the country in which we live. A magical mosaic.

Great stories from all around our world provide the backdrop.

Greek and Roman heroes, gods battling with fierce creatures and awesome natural disasters. Hercules, Theseus, Venus, Zeus, Alexander the Great and Caesar.

Add the legends of the Far and Middle East. Aladdin, the Pharaohs of Egypt, the fearsome Moghul Hordes

Mix in the stories from the great religions. Adam and Eve, Noah, Moses, Lord Buddha and Rama.

The legends created in our small patch of land, these catch our attention at the heart of the mosaic.

Viking Raiders. Thor and Woden. The magic of King Arthur and his heroic Knights. Then Kings and Queens in battle. Great empires and brave deeds. Great givers to others and great artists. Shakespeare, Robin Hood, Queen Elizabeth I, Nelson, Florence Nightingale, Elgar, the Rolling Stones.

We immerse ourselves in these tales and they make us feel good. They give us a sense of belonging. And most especially when we go the place where the legend was created. Visit Tintagel, listen to the Arthurian stories, see the grandeur, breathe the magic. Read Wuthering Heights. Roam the Yorkshire Moors. Feel the magical power of nature. Immerse yourself in the stories of Robin Hood. Go visit the Major Oak in Sherwood Forest. Go to Plymouth. Look out to sea and feel what Francis Drake felt over four hundred years ago.

Breathe deeply. Let the magic in. Find your own inner hero.

That's what this group of stories is all about. They focus on one part of our country. The beautiful Surrey Hills. The stories don't just focus on the beauty of the Hills. That you can find in many other books. These stories tell you about how you are going to feel when you visit the Surrey Hills. They do this by telling the stories of all kinds of living beings who have found heroism in the Hills. They overcome huge challenges, and become Surrey Hills SuperHeroes.

The stories borrow and adapt from many sources. The stories are not restricted by time and space. They are a fusion of history, legend, truth and fiction. They adapt ideas from all eras; gods and goddesses; heroes and heroines in the Classics; the myths and folktales of recent history through to the issues we all talk about today. They have one thing in common. They all have a link to the Surrey Hills and they all talk of things we need to do to sustain the beauty of the Hills.

We hope you will be entertained by these stories. We hope you will read them yourself, read them to your children and get your children to read them.

These stories have been developed, written, illustrated and published by people living and working in the Surrey Hills. People who believe that local employment is important and that attracting others to visit the Hills, either physically or in their imaginations, will generate local jobs. People who also believe that sustaining the beauty of the Hills is essential for those who live in the Hills as well as those who might visit.

We hope these stories will inspire you to visit the Surrey Hills, and enjoy some of the places we have written about and illustrated. When you visit, plunge yourself into the experience, and the magic, that the Hills offer.

So, head for the Hills, set your mind free, and breathe deeply. You may well find your own inner SuperHero. We think you will, and we hope you agree that, in the end, everything is magic.

Steve Markwell and Cathy Coleman

THE DINOSAURS OF THE SURREY HILLS

Long, long ago, dinosaurs ruled the whole world, and in this story, we meet a family of them who lived in the beautiful place we now call the Surrey Hills. You will also learn interesting things about the Hills which you can still explore today.

Meet the mother dinosaur, Gertrude, and the father dinosaur, Montmorency the First, and their two boys. The older brother is called Montmorency the Second, and the younger Montmorency the Third. You see, their parents both liked the name Montmorency very much, and long ago there weren't as many names as we have today, so they decided to stick with a name they liked.

The family was happy. They loved exploring the area around their home. There was only one problem for Gertrude and Montmorency the First. Their two sons kept arguing and squabbling. About absolutely nothing, and absolutely everything. They argued about which part of a log they should sit on. They argued about what they wanted to eat for lunch. They argued about how deep a river was, how cold it might be, and how many fish were in the water.

They didn't take things seriously. They needed to grow up. They drove Gertrude and Montmorency the First stark, staring bonkers!

Then Gertrude came up with a brilliant idea. "Listen dear Montmorency the First," she said, "we need to turn this arguing and squabbling into something they can enjoy, something that gets them excited, and most importantly, something that tires them both out!"

So, Montmorency the First put together a big competition for his sons. A sort of World Cup or Olympics for young dinosaurs.

His sons needed to compete against each other in four big events; wrestling, wading in the river, football, and rock throwing.

The boys loved it.

They started with the wrestling. With all their energy they grappled and shoved, tripped each other up and fell on each other. After three days of exhausting wrestling, Montmorency the First declared the result a draw.

The next competition was the wading. They jumped into the River Wey and began the race towards what we now call the River Thames. For hours, Montmorency the Second led the race, and it looked like he was going to win, but then the more energetic Montmorency the Third put on a last-minute burst of speed and again... it was a draw.

The football match was played on the vast open grasslands where Stoke Park in Guildford is today. Dinosaurs from all over Surrey came to watch. It was a fearsome game, with huge kicks and tough tackles. Montmorency the Second scored first. Then Montmorency the Third used his speed to score three goals in a row. After 8 hours of play, it was getting dark, and

Montmorency the Second was leading five goals to four. In the last minute, a penalty to Montmorency the Third. GOALLLLLLL!!!

Once again, a draw. It was now all down to rock throwing.

The rules were simple. The brothers had to stand at least fifteen miles apart. The first to hit the other with a rock was the winner. For safety, Gertrude made both sons wear huge helmets and padded clothing.

Montmorency the Second stood near where Hindhead is today. Montmorency the Third near Albury.

Montmorency the Second threw first. He missed his brother by miles. His rock landed in Painshill Park, near where the lake is today.

Montmorency the Third threw next. His rock landed far away from where his brother was standing. It crashed into the ground where the Devil's Punchbowl is today.

Montmorency the Second's next throw smashed into the ground between Newlands Corner and Shere. It made a very big dent in the ground, about where Silent Pool is today.

Just as Montmorency the Third was about to throw again, his brother called out in a very loud voice.

"Stop" he shouted, "did you see where that last rock landed? That hole is enormous! We're breaking up the hills!". Montmorency the Third looked around, and saw that a lot of the other dinosaurs who had been watching them were looking nervous, almost scared, wondering where the next rock would land. "You're right" he replied, "maybe this has gone too far; we should be looking after our beautiful home and making sure there is still a beautiful home here for everyone".

So, the two brothers put down their rocks and went home. From then on they treated the Surrey Hills more as a home than an arena. They worked hard to make sure it was protected. And they made Gertrude and Montmorency the First the happiest, proudest parents, in all the dinosaur world.

There are places mentioned in this story that are well worth a visit: -

The River Wey. *If you join the towpath at Godalming, you can walk all the way to Weybridge where the Wey meets the Thames.*

Stoke Park *is in the middle of Guildford. It's a beautiful green space with many attractions, including a wonderful outdoor Lido.*

Newlands Corner *gives great views over the Hills. You can walk to the mystical* **Silent Pool**, *and the classic English villages of* **Shere** *and* **Albury***.*

Painshill Park *is a landscaped area of great beauty near Cobham. Look out for a giant cedar tree they say is the largest in Europe.*

The Devil's Punchbowl *is a huge park near Hindhead. Great walking.*

I hope you explore some of these. Wherever you go, look out for things that could be the work of dinosaurs!

There are a huge number of books about dinosaurs, and masses of information on the web.

There's an interesting folk tale called How the Devil's Jumps and the Devil's Punch Bowl came to be. You can find it in Surrey Folk Tales by Janet Dowling. 2013.

There are lots of stories about the Devil's Punchbowl. One relates to an argument between the devil and the god Thor, in which rocks are thrown. Find out more at www.nationaltrust.org.uk/hindhead-common-and-the-devils-punchbowl.

VESTA GODDESS OF FIRE

This story is about Vesta, her amazing powers, and her connection with the Surrey Hills.

Vesta was born with two huge powers. KAPOW! - Vesta creates fire. KAPOW! – Vesta freezes fire.

This story describes one of Vesta's greatest challenges, and tells how the goddess became a Surrey Hills SuperHero.

The universe was created by a huge explosion of fire and heat beyond anything we can imagine today. And then planets were created, out of fire and ice, heating and cooling, shrinking and expanding. Today our planet is still shaped by fire and ice, and the basic elements of water, earth, air and wind.

The Goddess Vesta was created at the same time as our planet. She was created with wonderful powers, able to harness the power of fire and use it to help develop Planet Earth.

If a fire became too hot, she had the power to cool it. If a fire got out of control, she could freeze the flames. Can you imagine that? A raging fire suddenly becoming a ring of frozen flames! Instead of allowing fire to destroy, Vesta could redirect its power to help develop our beautiful planet, as a force for good. Fire guided and directed by the Goddess Vesta.

Vesta worked long and hard until the planet cooled; water settled into clouds, rivers and oceans, and life began to appear: first plants, then life in the vast oceans, then life on land. Finally, humans like us appeared, to discover an amazing, beautiful place to live. With the arrival of humans, Vesta realized two very important things. Firstly, she had become exhausted by all her work over millions of years; every time she froze flames, she used up enormous amounts of energy. She was tired, and needed to rest for a long, long time. With sadness, she realized that now she would need to rest almost every time she used her powers. Her days of unending energy were over. But the need for her work was not over. Fire would always be present on the planet. It would always be a source of power, but also a source of destruction.

Vesta also realised that she could no longer work alone. Could humans help? She knew that humans could never have powers like hers. But they could be trained to make sure that fire was always used for good and that its destructive side never got out of control?

And so, Vesta went on an enormous journey. She travelled the whole planet. She travelled on foot, she travelled by horse and donkey and she even travelled by camel. She travelled on rafts, canoes, rowing boats and sail boats. She visited every land she could in our beautiful planet. And everywhere she visited, she found humans who understood the world as she understood it. Humans who cared for the world, and for all the living things in the world. Humans who wanted to build a good life for their children, not destroy things forever.

She met men and women who worked with natural things and worked hard. She met farmers, fishermen and women, bakers and cooks, housebuilders, even storytellers! She told them that she was organising a big meeting. At the meeting she would explain everything she had learned about fire, its power to help life, and its power to destroy life. Vesta invited all the humans who listened to her and understood her message. The meeting would happen in a place that Vesta had often visited. A place that she thought particularly beautiful. A place that, because of all the trees that grew there, could be damaged by fire. That place was The Surrey Hills.

And so, people from all over the planet who cared about preserving the beauty of our home journeyed to the Surrey Hills. A great meeting place was set up in a clearing on the top of a hill, now known as St Martha's. All the people sat on fallen tree trunks, or bales of hay specially prepared by local farmers. As you can imagine, with so many people in a beautiful place, there was much chatter, conversation and general hub-bub.

Vesta knew she had to get everyone's attention quickly, or the whole meeting could descend into a huge chaotic party. She had prepared something which she now put into action. In front of her, and right in the middle of the clearing, Vesta had built a big pile of dried wood. Using her magical powers, she set fire to the pile. KAPOW! KAPOW! The flames took hold immediately. The wood crackled and burnt fiercely, and the flames began to reach into, and burn the branches of the trees above the fire. The raging flames and heat got the attention of everyone in the crowd. An air of panic crept in. What if the fire got out of control, and people got burnt? The people at the back of the gathering began to leave. "If we don't run, we will all be burnt!" a voice cried out. In instant response, Vesta shouted out. "There is no need to panic!!" And KAPOW! KAPOW! – using her magical power, Vesta froze all the flames. In that second, Vesta had everyone's attention. The crowd looked at her in awe, and in silence.

"This fire is now under my control," said Vesta in a commanding voice. "But there are many, many fires on the planet that I cannot control" she said. "That is why I called you all here today. I have a job to offer you all. It is a very big job which I will explain to you. It may be that the job is too difficult for many of you. It is up to each of you to decide. Only accept if you are prepared to put all of your effort, all of your strength, all of your courage into the task. We will see, during this gathering, which of you has the power and strength to do the job.

I need to explain. This planet was born in fire. Without fire and heat, there would be no planet, so no mankind. Fire is a great gift to mankind. It is a source of many good things. Without fire, mankind could not warm their homes. Without fire, mankind could not heat and bend metal to make horseshoes and tools to dig the soil. But fire is also very dangerous to mankind, and to all living things on the planet. When fire is out of control, it can destroy whole forests, whole villages. It can destroy the people living in the villages. It can destroy all living things in the forest. I am the Goddess Vesta. I was created at the same time as the planet.

My job was to use the power and energy of fire to create a beautiful planet. It was also to make sure that fire did not destroy the beauty of nature. I had to ensure fire was always used for good. I was given special powers, as you have seen. I have had to use those powers many times, over thousands of years, to ensure a beautiful planet. But today I am tired and weary. I still have the power to create and to freeze flames. But now, when I use the power, I cannot use it again until I have rested for a long time. So, I need to find others, humans who I can work with, and then they can be my team all around the world and help make sure fire is used wisely. So, this is what we will do…"

Vesta's words were interrupted before she could finish. A young boy ran into the clearing and shouted at the top of his voice. "Fire! Fire! In Ripley! Huge Fire in Ripley!! Help!! Everything and everyone will be destroyed. Help! Help!!"

The meeting fell into chaos. "Ripley village is only 5 miles from here," a voice cried. "Let's run before we are caught in the fire."

"He's right," called out another. "It's woodland all the way between here and Ripley. It will catch like tinder. Let's get out of here."

Then Vesta's voice again, clear and commanding above the chaos "Stop. The first rule of fire is DO NOT PANIC. The second is ALWAYS SEEK TO HELP YOUR FELLOW HUMANS."

Sadly, Vesta's words fell on many deaf ears. Almost half the people left, running this way and that, in total fear of a huge fire.

Once they had left, Vesta set about organising everyone who remained into teams. One group was given the job of finding buckets in all the local farms and bringing them to Ripley as quickly as possible. Another group looked for tools to knock down buildings and trees, and so create a gap over which the fire could not jump. A third group was sent to find the nearest source of water in the area of Ripley, so that water to control the flames could be fetched. Vesta found a horse and raced to Ripley, the young man who had raised the alert, riding behind her.

Vesta and her team spent a long, hot, exhausting afternoon in Ripley, fighting the fire. They knocked down buildings and chopped down trees to stop the fire spreading. They formed a human chain

to get buckets of water from the river to help put out the flames. They helped people who had lost their homes to find shelter for the night. Vesta found out the fire had been caused by someone lighting a fire to cook some meat much too close to an old dried out building. She called all the townsfolk together to tell them they must be much more careful with fire in the future.

When the work was done, Vesta and her team of fire fighters went back to St Martha's to rest and eat. She talked to them again. "We have done good work today. We have saved Ripley from burning down completely and we have saved many lives, many trees and wild animals. And we have all learned many things. You all have learned how to respect and control fire. I have learned that you people who helped me fight the fire are worthy to form my team of helpers. Not those who ran away and panicked. So, I name you all "Surrey Hills SuperHeroes." Using my magical powers, I will talk with all of you in the future, wherever you live. You must help people who live around you, to use fire sensibly. You must help them when an unwanted fire breaks out. You must call me if you have a big problem. And trust me, I will call you when I need help from you all. We are going to be busy!"

———————⚫———————

St Martha's Hill and Church make a marvellous trip out. You can climb the steep hill and reach St Martha's church. The view from the top of the Hill is stunning.

Ripley is a charming village in the Surrey Hills that has existed since Norman times.

The village has some marvellous old coaching inns. Now often great cafes, pubs and restaurants. Ripley is close to the River Wey, and to the Royal Horticultural Gardens at Wisley, both great places to walk and explore.

Every month, there is an excellent Farmers Market on the green.

In 1969, a great fire destroyed several properties in Ripley, and further damage was only prevented by the good work of Surrey Fire services.

THE GREEN MAN

Amy Elizabeth was looking for bluebells. They always bloomed in May, covering the slopes of the Surrey Hills in a soft electric blue and magically lighting up the shadows cast by the branches of trees. Soft, inviting, calm, inspiring, with a waft of sweet perfume. She had wandered a little way away from her family in her search, but she could still hear their voices from the other side of the slope she was exploring. She soon found a small clump of bluebells. One or two outliers, right beside the trodden path. Then, a dozen steps later, a multitude, covering the whole slope. As far as she could see, and exclusively for her.

She hesitated before calling the others; she delighted in being alone in nature, breathing deeply, with the heady mix of the sights and smells all to herself. She was about to shout out to the others to come and share her find but suddenly her attention was diverted by a noise from the opposite direction of her group, something deeper in the forest. A rustling of leaves. The faint sound of a tread on soft earth. Then a whisper, almost a mumble on the slight breeze. She thought she heard the words "Morpeth", and then "Norwich": towns she had enjoyed visiting with her family. But perhaps her ears played tricks. She peered through the branches. She thought she saw a large shadowy object in the distance, moving slowly from tree to tree. Her senses were alive, but she was not afraid. There seemed no hint of menace or threat in the forest. On the contrary, she was intrigued, eager to find the source of the sounds.

She followed a winding path; the earth was soft underfoot and branches thick with new leaves cast shadows over her path, with bluebells spreading out either side. She came across a fallen old beech tree, and with banked earth either side of her path she had to crawl underneath. Still determined to find the source of the noise, she got on all fours and crawled under, taking care not to bump her head or spoil her hair with earth or twigs. Her hair, long, dark, and shiny, was very important to her. She got through without a problem, pausing just to shake off any offending leaves from her hair. Then she looked up. There, no more than fifteen paces in front of her, was a large figure, perhaps three metres tall. He was looking down, a faint smile in his hooded eyes, and whispering softly to a leaf springing from a twig near his head.

This was a remarkable figure. Half man, half tree. His head was large, made larger by a huge mass of curly, unruly hair, which reached almost to his shoulders. His body was in proportion to his height. Broad, muscular shoulders, powerful looking arms and legs, large feet without socks or boots planted firmly on the forest floor. He was dressed in soft green jacket and trousers. The fabric was woven, tough and worn. But perhaps the most remarkable feature of this figure was the face. It was gnarled and worn, like an old oak. It was imposing, with hooded eyes that seemed to see and understand everything. It was at the same time a face that carried a wry and warm smile. The most amazing feature of this face were vines, which seemed to emerge from the ears of this huge figure.

"Hello, and what is your name young lady?" The voice was deep and rough, but warm and non-threatening.

"My name is Amy Elizabeth," said the girl, in a quiet, confident voice.

"Well, that's extraordinary," came the reply. "I meet so few people with two names. You see my name is Green Man. So, I'm like you, you see, two names. And…"

"Before we get into all that, and start discussing the history of names, I would like to know what you are doing here," Amy Elizabeth cut in, afraid that otherwise she would lose the whole day in idle chatter.

"Well that," said the Green Man, "is quite a story."

"And I would very much like to hear it," she replied. "But I don't have all day, not even all morning for that matter. So, I suggest you get on with it, so I can hear it before my family arrive."

"Then I suggest we make ourselves comfortable," said the Green Man. "Why don't you climb up on the old beech tree and sit there. That way we'll be closer to the same height, and I won't have to shout. I will stand beside you and lean against this fine oak." He indicated a big branch of the oak tree. "I will use this branch for support. That way any bird or forest creature who wants to talk to me, can perch on the branch and communicate without difficulty."

Amy Elizabeth raised her eyebrows at the thought of small birds talking to this green giant. She said nothing, out of fear of stopping the story that was about to unfold.

"I am the Green Man. Some have called me "Jack the Green," and some have even thought I was Robin Hood. But his is quite another story.

I am the guardian of the forest. I have been charged, from the start of all creation, with the task of ensuring that the forest thrives and stays healthy. The forest is home to many plants and creatures.

It provides shelter and food for them. So, in addition to caring for the trees, I need to help maintain a good relationship between all the living things that exist here. It is a really important job. You see, trees literally bind everything on the Earth together."

"Do you have to do this all on your own?" Amy Elizabeth chipped in.

"No. I have responsibility for the wonderful Surrey Hills. But there are others elsewhere, many others, who help in many ways."

"Do they all have two names?" Amy Elizabeth had a wry grin on her face.

"No, not at all, some have…." The Green Man stopped in mid-sentence. Partly because he realized he was being teased, and partly because a robin was saying something in his ear.

The Green Man finished the conversation with the robin. Then turned again to Amy Elizabeth. "You are so sharp, young lady, you might just cut yourself! I will have to be careful about what I say to you. But to continue with my serious story, there are many like me all around the world. There are others too, in the Surrey Hills, who care for the water, and try to keep fire under control. Perhaps we will talk of them later."

"Have you had your job long?" Asked Amy Elizabeth. "I must say, by the condition of your clothes, it may be time you retired."

By now, the Green Man had learned to ignore Amy Elizabeth's little jokes.

"I started my work nearly three hundred and seventy million years ago" said the Green Man. I have been guardian of the forest ever since. There have been many, many problems along the way. But I'm happy to say, that up until recently, I have been able to help overcome them all."

Amy Elizabeth noted a change in the Green Man, as he said these words. A sadness overcame his face. She was about to ask what it was that had happened recently, when a squirrel descended from the oak, dug an old acorn out of the Green Man's hair, and whispered a few words in his ear. She was sure that she would hear of "recent problems" later. So, once the squirrel had departed, and the Green Man had wiped a tear from under his eye, she allowed the story to continue.

"Oh yes, where was I? Problems to overcome from the start. That's it. Did you know," he said "that tree like plants first emerged from the water three hundred and seventy million years ago. That's when I arrived. And straight away, we started trying to build forests. The first problem to solve was that the stems of the plants that emerged, were weak and floppy. You see, they were used to living in the water. So, they had nothing like the strength or size of this huge oak, that I am leaning on. It took me a long, long time to work with these plants, and build their strength, and make them strong and robust like the forest you see around you.

In all this work, I was sharing my experiences with other guardians of the forest, all around this wonderful planet of ours. If we hadn't worked as a team, I don't know what kind of state we would be in now. As time went by, living things began to use the trees as a home, and play their part in the development of the great forests. Like spiders, insects, centipedes and millipedes, who also helped to regenerate the forest around trees that had died and fallen."

Amy Elizabeth shuddered at the mention of spiders. Spiders falling into her hair was her worst nightmare. She was determined, however, not to show her fear to the Green Man.

"Animals and birds too made their home here. I learned to speak their languages, to show them that I was their friend. That way, I could show them the best places to live, and help avoid overcrowding in any part of the forest. Keeping all their food supplies in balance is very important you see. Yes, balance in everything, that's my motto. Balance in everything."

And then," said the Green Man thoughtfully, a frown on his brow, "mankind appeared in the woods."

"You say that," said Amy Elizabeth "in a way that makes me think that perhaps you don't like mankind so much."

"There are many things that happen on this planet that at first, perhaps, you don't like so much. The thing is, I have had to learn to accept changes as they happen. Then find out the good things that come with the changes, and make the very best of them."

There was a pause after the Green Man said these words. Both he and Amy Elizabeth were deep in thought for a few moments.

A ray of sunlight broke through the overhanging branches, throwing illumination on the Green Man's face, at once friendly and careworn.

"I have worked with mankind from the start. When I first saw man, I reminded myself of something my old friend Eleanor the Invisible told me; "Do not be inhospitable to strangers. They may be angels in disguise." So, I showed mankind the best timber to cut, and how to shape it to build shelters. Mankind hunted for food in the forest. I talked to them about keeping things in balance. Not hunting animals or gathering berries in a way that caused the destruction of the very things that provided them food. At the beginning of every new year, I work with the trees and plants in the forest to make sure Spring arrives. When the new leaves and plants arrive, and flowers like your bluebells blossom, I help organise big celebrations with mankind in the Surrey Hills.

I have worked with mankind long and hard to combat disease in the woods. Yes, disease among the trees is a major problem. Ash and box are having problems right now. I have shown mankind how to plant new trees where old trees have fallen or been cut down. It is so important to keep a mix of tree types in the forest. This increases resistance to disease. It's also better to plant new trees that are native to the area. Bringing in new trees from outside the Hills can bring in disease. Use fire with great caution and respect. Fire is a great gift to mankind, offering warmth and light. Wrongly used, most especially in the forest, it is a terrible threat. Can you imagine the destruction? The suffering and death among all living things? Worst of all, some fires are man-made. So, I tell all humans "Be careful with fire in the forest. Do not idly throw lighted matches around. Do not bring your cooking fires into the forest!" And most of mankind does listen to me, and sees the sense of my words."

"So," said Amy Elizabeth, "I think we should all congratulate and thank you for your marvellous work. All of us. Trees, plants, insects, birds, animals, mankind. We should all thank you for a job well done and listen to your wise words."

"Your thoughts are kind," replied the Green Man. "But I think your thanks are given too soon. You see, there is one problem that neither I, nor any of my friends across the planet, have been able to solve. It is a serious one too."

"When I first saw you, in the distance, across the field of bluebells, I heard you muttering some things that I could not hear perfectly. Was it this problem you were talking about?" asked Amy Elizabeth.

"I'm not sure," said the Green Man. "What do you think I was saying?"

"I think you were saying the names of two towns I have visited. Both have lots of trees near them, so maybe it makes sense. What I think I heard was "Morpeth and Norwich.""

The Green Man reflected for a few seconds, pulling on one of the vines that came from his ear. Then "No I wasn't saying the names of towns. I was saying "No more gifts. No more gifts. Please, no more gifts."

"No more gifts," said Amy Elizabeth. "What kind of a story is that?"

"It is a sad and frustrating story," replied the Green Man, "and it's about the serious problem we were talking about. I am almost embarrassed to speak of it."

"Please tell it to me," said Amy Elizabeth. "I may be able to help. Unless of course the story concerns people with two names."

The Green Man ignored the teasing, and his face remained glum as he started describing the problem. "For a long time, kind people have given me presents at the Spring festivals. Not many presents, but always much appreciated. A flower garland for my hair. A new woven shirt. Then, about ten, or perhaps fifteen years ago, people started leaving me presents on the forest floor. Sometimes hanging on tree branches. Cups for me to drink from. Beautiful, printed boxes for me to store things in. Shiny decorations for

the twigs on the trees, or the flowers. Of course, I gathered the presents, and took them back to the place where I shelter.

I try to gather them all up, but there are so many. I hardly have room to store them all anymore. And the forest begins to look untidy. I'm sure it's not good for the plants and animals. I don't want to seem ungrateful, but I really need the present giving to stop. All I know is that a lot of the cups left for me seem to be presents from American visitors. I am sure that the boxes for storing my things are made in Italy. The shiny decorations I think come from energetic dog walkers! It's all too much! No more gifts please. No more gifts."

The Green Man was almost in tears. Amy Elizabeth stopped the story. "Can you show me examples of these gifts, please?"

The Green Man nodded. From a pocket, he produced one of the cups he had talked about. He reached around the back of the tree and found an example of a "beautifully printed storage box." Then he looked down, and saw a shiny piece of decoration, lying half covered by bluebells. He summoned a squirrel, who ran down, picked up the decorative material in its teeth, then presented it to Amy Elizabeth.

She examined all three items. She smiled, more in embarrassment than amusement.

"Here's the thing, my Green Man friend," she said. "This cup isn't a present from a visitor from America. It says "Americano Coffee" on the cup. Someone has drunk the coffee and thrown the cup away. The storage boxes aren't for your things, and they are definitely not from Italy. They are empty pizza boxes people have left in the forest. And the shiny decorations from energetic dog walkers? I'm sorry to tell you they are simply empty hot dog wrappers. Not presents to decorate the forest."

The Green Man's jaw fell. His head dropped. Two more acorns fell from his hair.

"I hate to tell you, but all these things are not gifts at all. They are rubbish that has been thrown away," said Amy Elizabeth.

The Green Man was distraught. "Rubbish" he cried. "Thrown away in this beautiful forest! The slubberdegullions!" he shouted.

Amy Elizabeth, anxious to break the thunderous mood of the giant, asked the obvious question. "Whatever is a slubberdegullion?"

"A nasty, dirty fellow who would wilfully destroy beauty," roared the Green Man. "I will catch them all and hang them up in the trees!"

"Now, now," said Amy Elizabeth. "Your anger will solve nothing. We don't want to stop people coming to the forests and having a good time there. We just want them to take their rubbish home with them. I have a solution to suggest."

The Green Man stopped shouting and looked at Amy Elizabeth carefully.

"First, I will gather my family and my friends, and clean up the forest with you. We will find everything the slubberdegullions have left. Then we will load it into my dad's enormous four-wheel drive, and we will take it to the proper place for re-cycling."

"That's wonderful," said the Green Man. "But then the slubberdegullions will be back with more rubbish!"

"That's the next part of my campaign. We are going to make you a Surrey Hills SuperHero on social media. You will become a famous giant who stops people from throwing litter. You will become an influencer to stop littering."

The Green Man cut in quickly. "I don't like this social media thingummy. I will have none of it."

The reply was instant. "There are many things that happen on this planet that at first, you don't like so much. The thing is, you have to learn to accept changes as they happen. Then find out the good things that come with the changes and make the very best of them."

The Green Man knew he had met his match.

"Here is what we will do. First, we will agree a date when my family, and all my friends, will come back, and clean the forest with you. And right now, I will take a picture of you with my brand-new iPhone, that I'm sure you already detest! By the miracle of modern technology, I'm going to make your photo a little less frightening. I'm going to give you a super new cape. The cape is going to be a be in green, a bit brighter than the one you wear today. The cape will be trimmed with the electric blue of my favourite flower. I will trim your hair and beard, even your vine leaves a little. I will post the photo on social media. Don't worry, it will still be you. You will become a Surrey Hills SuperHero leading the whole world in a fight against litter in the forest."

The Green Man looked as though he had a thousand questions.

"Don't worry. It will work. Everyone will listen to a three-metre giant who has been around for millions of years. But now, I must go. I can just see my cousin coming down the path. I have to crawl back under the beech tree."

"Make sure no spiders or creepy crawlies fall into that lovely hair!"

Amy Elizabeth knew she had made a friend who really understood her.

She crawled through, stood up and looked back. The Green Man had disappeared. Walking towards her was her cousin Matt.

"Where have you been?" said Matt. "I'm sure I heard you talking to somebody."

"I've just been admiring the bluebells."

"What bluebells?" said Matt, with a grin.

"Oh Matt. You are such a boy!"

"But seriously Amy Elizabeth, who were you talking to?" replied Matt.

"Check out my Facebook post Matt. Then you'll know."

———————•———————

*Bluebells bloom in the Surrey Hills between late April and end May. They carpet the Surrey woodlands with an amazing electric blue. **Leith Hill, Gatton Park, Reigate Hill**, and **Box Hill** are particularly good places to view the bluebell show. And hopefully, to admire the work of the Green Man and Amy Elizabeth.*

If you want to follow up on the Green Man, there is a huge amount of background material. Just Google Green Man, and study all the links on Wikipedia.

ELEANOR THE INVISIBLE

Eleanor the Invisible is a story inspired by the legends that surround the mystical Silent Pool. This pool in the heart of the Surrey Hills is well worth visiting. The scenery is stunning. Near the pool, you will find lots of local artisanal products. A distillery, a vineyard, a local cheese maker, and a restaurant and shop selling authentic Indian dishes. Close by are classic English villages: Albury, Shere and Abinger Hammer. The wide, breathtaking views from Newlands Corner and St Martha's are within walking distance.

This is a story about water, most particularly, fresh water. Eleanor tells us how important clean, fresh water is to everyone. There are many places in the Surrey Hills where there are beautiful stretches of fresh water. The Wey, the Tillingbourne,the River Mole, Godstone Pond, Frensham Ponds, the flooded quarry at Buckland and of course, Silent Pool.

ELEANOR'S STORY

I was born more than seven hundred years ago, the youngest child in a family who lived near Silent Pool in the Surrey Hills. My father was a woodcutter; my mother worked for the local miller, helping him grind corn for bread. My brother William was the first born. My sister Emma came next. And Eleanor the baby of the family - that's me.

Both my parents worked so hard: my father out in all weathers, searching for trees that needed cutting down, then working on them with his sharp axe, cutting and chopping the wood into logs, then hauling the logs on a sled to a place of shelter, sometimes pulling the sled himself, sometimes borrowing a local farmer's horse. When the wood was dry, my father could sell some of the logs to local farmers, often in exchange for food. Most of the wood, however, had to be given to the local lord. He owned the land where my father worked. If we were lucky, there were logs left over to keep our small two-roomed cottage warm in winter.

For my mother, it was hard, heavy work at the mill. Dangerous too. If the corn got too hot between the grinding stones, it could burst into flames and cause terrifying fires. She also helped the local baker, and sometimes brought home a delicious warm loaf.

My brother was a strapping boy, full of energy. He loved to help my father. He would run through the forest looking for trees that were ready to be felled. Then, at the end of the day, helping my father drag the wood back to shelter. When he grew up, he became a soldier earning his living by fighting for kings, lords and dukes all across Europe. He married a Spanish lady from Barcelona, and raised a family with her by the Mediterranean Sea.

My sister Emma. Ah yes, Emma, the famous one in our family. She loved adventure: full of daring, aways laughing, always exploring the Surrey Hills and forests. Everyone knows her story, so I won't tell it now. If you want to find out about Emma, visit Silent Pool.

Then the baby of the family. Me. Eleanor. Named after a famous Queen of England. People said that I was the quiet, thoughtful child. I know I wasn't as daring as Emma or as noisy. For as long as I can remember, I was interested in the living things in the forest: I loved to study the rhythm of nature; the changing of the seasons; the heat of summer which made me seek the cool of the forest;

the wonderful sounds of birdsong and bees looking for flowers; the gifts of Autumn, the berries which ripened and the excitement of harvest. Then the magic of the leaves turning colour, the biting cold of winter winds, snow on the ground and ice on the water, and finally, Spring, my favourite season of all: the arrival of the bluebells in the forest; the leaves beginning to show on the twigs of trees; birdsong back in the forest.

So, this was how I passed my time. I spent it in quiet study, not like my noisy brother and sister. I was at home in nature. Water was the part of nature that attracted me most. I loved to explore the pools and streams that were near to my home. The beautiful Tillingbourne river, which winds through the valley bottom. The mysterious Silent Pool, with its greeny-blue water. The Sherbourne Pool, lower down. I loved clear, fresh water. I felt I could almost talk to it, and it could talk to me. I understood the rhythm of water. I knew when a storm was coming long before it rained. I sensed when streams were drying up and lakes and pools were being starved of life-giving refreshment. I had never seen the sea, but I adored the tales seafarers told when they passed through our village. The idea of the power of huge waves and currents and tides excited me.

Unlike my brother and sister, I had no fear of water. I loved to bathe in fresh cool water, particularly in Sherbourne Pool. When I was immersed in water, I became totally relaxed. A quiet buzzing filled my head, ZZZZZZZZZ…. almost as if I was dropping to sleep.

I was bathing in Sherbourne Pool one day in late Spring, my favourite time. The weather had warmed enough to make it pleasant. Then something happened to make that day one of the most significant in all my long life.

At first, I had been splashing and kicking and diving. Afterward, I lay back and floated, enjoying the quiet. ZZZZZZZZ…..Then, in the distance, I heard a faint drumming. The drumming grew louder and I recognized the sound of hoof beats. Horses approaching, and several by the sound of it. Then a shout and a cry. Men's voices, calling in excitement. Just like my brother and father called to each other in the forest. I felt no fear. Mostly because I was in water where I never felt fear. I had no place to run or hide anyhow. I was in the middle of the pond. I had to keep calm. The buzzing in my head grew louder – more insistent. ZZZZZZZZ………. . It wasn't scaring me, but rather it was making me concentrate on what was going on.

The hoofbeats and the cries were close now.

Suddenly a huge white charger broke through the woodland cover near the pond. On the back of the massive horse, a knight in shining armour. The sight of horse and rider filled my vision. The knight had a sword on his side. He carried an enormous shield decorated with a red lion on a background of green and yellow. Knight and horse paused at the edge of the pond. The knight looked over the pond, and then looked straight at me. I was strangely unafraid, and remembered something my mother often said. "Do not be unkind to strangers. They may be angels in disguise."

So, I raised an arm, and waved at the knight in greeting. He made no response. It was as if he hadn't seen me. He continued to gaze at the pond, then lifted his eyes to the hills beyond. More knights on horseback broke through the cover, and joined the leader. Soon there were at least twelve horses and riders at the poolside. No one gave me any recognition. There was a lot of conversation between the knights. They were seeking the best way to the sea, where they would take a boat to fight a war in foreign lands. I raised my hand in greeting again, even smiled. Nothing. It might as well have been invisible!

Then the first knight barked a command, and they rode off. I was left alone in the quiet pond. The buzzing in my head calmed. All sense of danger passed.

I got out of the pond, and ran as fast as I could to our home. There I found my mother. She had returned from the bakers, and had boiled a pot of water on the fire. She helped me dry, and gave me a

hot spiced drink, and a slice of delicious warm bread. When I was calm, I told my mother the whole story of the day's events. I was afraid she would be angry with me for putting myself in danger. But she listened carefully and calmly to every word. When I came to the part about the armed riders not seeing me in the pool, she showed no surprise.

At the end of the story, my mother said, "Now I must tell you a story that will help explain everything. Long, long ago, there was a woman called Melusine. She had the most marvellous magical gifts. She loved nature, and understood all the wonderful gifts it gave to mankind. And in particular she understood water, and its importance to all living things, especially mankind. It was said that she could talk to rivers and lakes, even to the seas. They too could talk to her. You and I are descended from Melusine. I have not told you this before, but I have many of the powers of my ancestor. You, Eleanor, are the only one of my children who has inherited all Melusine's magical powers. You must use them wisely, and we will talk about that."

I told my mother I still didn't understand why the knights had not seen me in the pond.

"Because of your magical powers, you become invisible when you are in water" my mother explained. "The water sees if you are in danger, and makes you invisible, to protect you. You are very important to water. Water knows that and protects you. When water is protecting you, a pleasant buzzing will fill your ears. If great danger approaches, the buzzing will be louder. It's a sign that water is protecting you at all times, so you don't panic if you see scary things."

That day I decided I would become Eleanor the Invisible, the Guardian of the Water in the Surrey Hills. I would use all the powers I had inherited to safeguard the wonderful fresh water of our Hills. It was my way of thanking water for the protection it gave me.

Since that fateful day, I have roamed the Surrey Hills, telling everyone how important fresh water is, how to respect it and use it well. I talk to everyone I meet. I tell them how water is esssential for the growing of food. How we can use it, with care, for power - like the stream that powers the mill where my mother helps grind corn. How we need it for drinking and keeping clean. I explain how we must treasure it. Never throw dirty things into pools or streams. How we must be very careful about stopping the water flowing freely, for fear of causing floods. I have put to good use my magical ability to talk with water. If I hear that there is a risk of floods, or that harmful things are being tipped into water or a big storm is coming, I tell the local people so they can work to stop bad things happening.

For a long time, I just worked in the Surrey Hills. Then one day I was talking to my friend the Green Man who is Guardian of the Forests. He told me that all across our planet, there was much work to be done to develop the supply of fresh water. I explained to the Green Man that there was only so far I could walk in a day. So, working across the whole planet was beyond me. He took me to a magician he knew. The magician made for me a lovely suit in forest green. He made me a cloak in the beautiful colours of the waters of Silent Pool. All made in the lightest material – like a spider's web. He made me strong boots, so I could work alongside others in the planet to keep fresh clean water flowing. Finally, he made me the

most amazing gloves. Between the thumbs and each of the fingers there was the material you see in spiders webs. All in a rainbow of colours. The gloves, the magician explained, would work like wings – they would make me fly.

The magic worked. From that day on, I have flown the world over. I have seen so many problems with keeping water clean and met so many people who have no fresh water at all. I have helped wherever I can. Wherever I fly to in my cape, strong boots and magical rainbow gloves, I am known as Eleanor the Surrey Hills SuperHero, Guardian of the Waters of the Planet" And when I bathe in the water, I become Eleanor the Invisible- ZZZZZZZZZZZZ.

Having water to protect you at all times is a wonderful gift. ZZZZZZZZ….. You will find out how important this is in other stories about me you can read.

WALLY THE WALRUS.

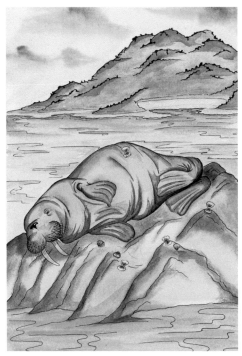

Some time ago, newspapers all across the world were reporting the story of a walrus who made a huge journey, visiting several European countries before heading back to the Artic. This walrus became known as Wally the Walrus. This story is based on those newspaper reports, although his travel plan has been changed a bit, and quite a few imaginary elements added, particularly the parts about him meeting Surrey Hills SuperHeroes.

Sadly, there are not so many walruses left in the world. So, a story that reminds us of how remarkable these mammals are, is probably a good idea. If you are wondering what a walrus has to do with the Surrey Hills, read on.

The story is told in Wally's words.

I remember well how my big adventure started. I was doing what I do best and love best. I was lying on the ice in the afternoon sun, dozing and snoring and dreaming of seafood. The day before, I had eaten the biggest and best seafood meal ever and I woke up thinking about getting ready to eat again.

I felt my ice bed bobbing around a bit. That's funny, I thought. That's never happened before. I lifted my head to take a look. When you are a walrus, lifting your head is a big effort because we have big heads and big tusks! Anyway, I did finally lift my head off the ice, and looked. What did I see? Big waves in the sea in front of me. So, I looked to one side, and what did I see? More big waves. And to the other side: big waves again. And finally, I heaved myself up on my flippers. And looked behind me. "Clams and crabs' legs!" I said to myself. (You humans say "Crumbs!" because you eat bread. Walruses say "Clams and crabs' legs" because we eat seafood). All I could see around me were waves. I was marooned on a small ice island. Behind me and disappearing quickly was my home, the frozen Artic Sea. I was drifting on a small piece of ice which had broken away. "Clams and crabs' legs," I cried out again. "Whatever shall I do? I need clams and tasty seafood to eat and a nice solid ice bed to sleep on. And I have none of those things here. I am just drifting in this huge sea."

And just when I was getting my tusks in a real twist, an Artic Tern landed on the ice beside me. "And what are you getting so tearful and wobbly about?" the bird asked me. I explained my problems. "I need rest and sleep and lots of seafood and clams to eat. But here I am alone and stranded on this tiny piece of ice drifting who knows where?"

"You have no need to worry," said the Artic Tern. "I myself travel huge distances every year from the Artic in the North to the Antarctic in the South. You just need to keep calm, follow your tusks and everything will work out just fine. I suggest you just rest on your little ice island, let it drift and wait until you see land. Then swim ashore and I know you will find lots of clams and seafood to eat and places to sleep." I had a thousand questions for this remarkable bird but before I could ask them, she was off on the wing.

I didn't have a better idea, so I did what she had told me. I lay dozing on my island, getting more and more hungry. Every time I dropped off to sleep, I dreamt of clams and shrimp and all manner of delicious sea food. I drifted and drifted and had no real idea where I was headed. Finally, after three hungry days and three hungry nights, I saw land in the distance. I was weak from lack of seafood but I was determined to get to ashore. So, I left my ice island home and jumped in the sea and swam. I finally reached a beach and I flopped on it and slept. I was woken up the next day by local fishermen, asking if I was all right. They told me I had landed in County Kerry in Ireland. And most important of all, they said they would show me where I could catch clams and other seafood and eat as much as I wanted. These kind fishermen jumped into their small fishing boat and told me to follow them. We reached a small cove. And there I found delicious clams and seafood that I could eat to my heart's and my tummy's' content!

I ate and slept and ate and slept for many days. Local people came to see me and marvel at my appetite and my tusks! Finally, I had eaten all the seafood in the cove and I knew it was time to move on from County Kerry.

Thanks to all the yummy seafood I had eaten, I was back on top swimming form, full of confidence and keen for new adventure. So, I waved a flipper at the lovely people of County Kerry and set off swimming in the sea. I decided to head south, as the fisherman had said the water gets warmer as you go in that direction. Warm water - that would be a new experience for me!

I swam and swam for days and nights. I saw big ferries, giant container boats, smaller fishing boats and beautiful brave little sail boats. When they saw me, people on board always greeted me with cheers and waves. That helped keep me going on my marathon swim. Finally, I saw land again, and swam up a long channel that led from the sea to a safe harbour. Along the channel, there were huge rocks. And each rock was covered with, guess what.... big yummy, tasty shellfish.

I ate and ate and then lay on a nice flat rock to doze in the sun. When I woke up, several fishermen were staring at me. One of them said something to me. I think it was a question. But it was in a language I had not heard before. "Clams and crabs' claws" I shouted out, "I'm sorry I can't understand what you are saying." Then, by a wave of a hand, a pointing of a finger, a snort, a clap of my flippers or a lift of my tusks, we began to communicate. I learned I had arrived on the west coast of France. So, the locals were speaking in French. The fishermen were delighted to welcome me and were sure I would become a big tourist attraction.

I spent several days in this wonderful fishing harbour. Until...... yes, you are right! I had eaten all the shellfish off all the rocks. By this time, I had learned to speak quite a lot of French, so I explained to my new friends that I wanted to start my homeward journey. I was becoming homesick. "More likely clam sick!" Said one of the fishermen with a big grin. I ignored him of course.

They showed me the direction I would have to swim, and suggested I follow their fishing fleet for as far as they travelled. We set off at night. It was a beautiful journey. The sea was calm and the stars filled the sky. We stayed close to the land and passed several lighthouses whose bright beams warned us of dangerous rocks closer to shore. As the dawn broke, the fishing fleet stopped and put out their nets. They all tooted loudly as I continued my journey alone. "Good luck with the fishing," I shouted back to them in my very best French!

I swam for a day and night and lost site of the shore. Then on the next morning, the dawn broke a fiery red. Soon huge dark clouds covered the sky. The soft breeze turned into a cold howling wind. The rain fell in torrents. The waves picked up and soon became towering mountains all around me. I was already tired from my long journey. I began to really struggle to keep my head above the water. My tusks became heavier and heavier and my head began to drop as the waves crashed down. "Crabs legs and sea cucumbers" I shouted out in the raging storm. "I think I'm in big trouble here!" But there was nobody to hear my cries.

The bigger the waves, the weaker I became, until gradually I began to give up swimming, my head dropped and I closed my eyes.

When I opened my eyes again, I was lying on a small beach. Thankfully I could feel sunshine warming me up. I was surrounded by a large group of people, who stared at me with amazement and amusement. I greeted them in my very best French. This caused further amazement as it turned out they were all English. They told me I had been washed up on the beach after a terrible storm. They were relieved I was still alive. "Me too!" I said.

They told me I had arrived on the Scilly islands. "By my tusks, that's a silly name," I told them. That got things off to a poor start. They explained that the islands were called Scilly - SCILLY, not SILLY. They said they were the most beautiful and peaceful islands in the world and I was lucky to have been washed up here

"Sounds ok but have you got any clams or seafood I can eat?" I asked a little abruptly. You see I was very hungry. By now, I had annoyed most of the onlookers who began to drift away. One kind lady remained. She was dressed in a most unusual way. A long flowing dress, sturdy boots and unusual gloves with webbing between the fingers. She said she would show me how to get to the harbour where she was sure I would find shellfish to eat. She told me not to be upset by the locals who were simply not used to having walruses washed up on the shore. She told me her name was Eleanor and she was on holiday on the islands. She asked me what my name was. I said "I don't have one. It's not normal for a walrus to have a name."

"Well you're not a normal walrus" she said "and I shall call you Wally".

Eleanor showed me how to swim round to the local harbour. There I found lots of beautiful boats moored up on the quayside. And much, much more importantly, I found masses of beautiful shellfish on the rocks that surrounded the harbour. I gorged and gorged and immediately became a tourist attraction. A big crowd formed on the harbour wall. They began to shout and wave and point at me. This frightened me a little. Then I heard a lady talking to the crowd, explaining to them who I was and what had happened to me. I was pretty sure it was Eleanor's voice. So, I carried on munching shellfish to my tummy's content.

By the time night fell, I had eaten my fill. "Crabs legs and clams" I said to myself "I need to find somewhere to sleep." There was certainly no comfy ice to lie on in the Scillies and the harbour rocks were jagged and not nice to sleep on. Then I had an idea. "By my tusks" I said "there are all these lovely boats in the harbour and nobody on them. I'm sure it will be okay if I clamber on to one and flop on the deck and snooze away." And that's what I did. As carefully as I could, (and I have to say that if you have tusks, it's difficult to be really careful) I clambered onto the biggest, finest boat and flopped down and dreamed of more clams than I had never dreamt of before.

I woke suddenly the next day. The sun was high in the sky. More importantly there was a large man with a very red face shouting at me. And he was armed with a long pole with a nasty looking metal hook at the end of it. "You ugly monster!" he shouted. "How dare you lie there on my beautiful boat! You have made a big mess. I am going to push you overboard." He thrust his pole aggressively towards me. "What have I done?" I asked, hoping to calm this red-faced man down.

"This is what you've done" shouted the man and he threw a newspaper at me. It was the Scilly Times. I could see the headline in huge red letters.

HUGE BEAST WRECKS BOATS IN HARBOUR

By this time a big crowd had gathered on the harbour wall.

"Push him into the water!" shouted one. "He's not from here and he speaks French." "Get rid of him!" cried another.

I was really frightened and thought my clam eating days were over.

Then suddenly, a strong voice at the back of the crowd said. "Stop this nonsense. We all need to talk sensibly. Let me through."

It was Eleanor. She forced her way through the crowd to the harbour wall and immediately commanded the crowd's attention. Even the angry red-faced man put down his pole.

"There are two or three things we all need to understand," said my friend Eleanor in a calm voice.

First, this is Wally the Walrus. There are not many walruses left in the world, so we should be kind and caring with Wally."

"The reason that Wally is here, is that the piece of ice he was living on in the Arctic broke off and drifted away. Believe me, I know all about water. Why it freezes and why it melts. So why did the ice break away? Because the ice started melting as the water got warmer. The world is getting warmer. We call it Global Warming. What we humans do contributes to Global Warming. But let's talk about what's important to people in the Scillies..."

"We need jobs!" shouted a voice on the wall.

"And what do we need for more jobs?" asked Eleanor.

"More tourists would help. Not broken boats!" shouted the red-faced man.

"So, I have to tell you that Wally is a major tourist attraction" said Eleanor. "He's in all the newspapers. He's famous!"

"He's famous for breaking boats!" shouted red faced man.

A voice came from the harbour wall. "I'm a carpenter. How about we all contribute a little and I can build Wally a nice raft to sleep on. I'll build a small Shepherd's Hut on the deck to shelter Wally with a sundeck in front of it. It will look really something! We will put the raft right where the restaurants and ice cream stands are. No more broken boats but lots of ice cream sales!"

Even the red-faced man thought this was a good idea. In fact, he bought his own ice cream stand on the strength of it. And the plan worked out for everyone.

After all the hubbub died down, Eleanor and I had a long chat. Eleanor told me that she had special powers that gave her a deep understanding of the power and importance of water.

Eleanor and water were able to communicate in a magical way. In fact, water could even protect her if she was in big danger, by making her invisible. Because of her remarkable clothing and particularly her amazing gloves, she was able to fly all over the world, helping those in need.

Her work had started in the Surrey Hills and so she was known as Eleanor the Invisible, Surrey Hills SuperHero.

"I've been talking to the other SuperHeroes" Eleanor told me "And we've all agreed to make you an honorary Surrey Hills SuperHero and give you this special Surrey Hills medal to wear around your neck."

"Look. I love the seafood here. And my new raft is an amazing place. I'm really pleased so many tourists are coming to see me and are buying ice cream. But I've done nothing to deserve this great SuperHero honour" I said.

"Oh yes you have" said Eleanor "you've been tough and courageous; you've worked hard and tried to understand people; you've even learned a different language. We think when people learn each other's languages it brings them together. We greatly admire these qualities in the Surrey Hills.

But if you accept this honour, we may call on you one day to help us. Someone will pass to you the secret code word SHISH!! and you must be ready for action."

"Crabs legs and clams" I said. "Whatever is this SHISH!! thing all about?"

"That" said Eleanor, "is the subject of a whole other story."

INTERVIEW WITH A DRAGON.

This is a story about a very special dragon. It shows another side to dragons, a little different from the one often portrayed in dragon stories.

I've always wanted a job that requires the combined talents of Graham Norton and David Attenborough. I love to interview people, and get them to tell me their stories, and I love working in the open air. This is an interview I did with a very unusual dragon, in a beautiful outdoor location….

I would like to be able to tell you it's a stunning start to the day. Warm, with a light, soft breeze. I would love to tell you I am enjoying the amazing view from my bench at Newlands Corner. The green valley below, with a light mist gradually lifting to reveal the cosy villages of Albury and Shere. Across the valley, the wooded hills rising again, inviting me to walk and explore their shaded mysteries. To the right, the top of Saint Martha's Church, destination for pilgrims and walkers and a legend for over a thousand years. I wish I could to tell you I can see all these things, and more. But this morning I can't; everywhere is completely grey, and cold and wet.

I can tell you though that all this makes me feel good. And you know what, I feel really great.

I can breathe and taste and smell the air of the Hills. Cold, fresh, slightly wooded and earthy. I hear the calm.

Inside, I feel as good as I think it's possible to feel. Inspired, relaxed, energy to get done what I want to get done. Energy is what I need, because today I have a big, demanding job. I have to interview Grace who is on a bench the other side of my picnic table. I have to get Grace to tell her stories, her challenges and her heroic deeds.

Grace is a dragon. She is a beautiful dragon. No intimidating attitude. No smelly fiery breath. No nasty scaly skin. She is very big, and at the same time soft and flexible. Long, supple neck. Powerful legs, with elegant claws. Massive wings, now neatly folded on the sides of her body. A sculpted head and jaw. Her skin is a beautiful hue of natural colours; her eyes a piercing green. She is calm, composed, attentive. She is ready to talk. I start with the obvious question.

"Why the name Grace? Not one normally associated with dragons."

"You know," says Grace "Dragons often get a very bad rap. Think about it. Most people see dragons as fierce, ugly and destructive. Full of attitude and aggression. The stories humans tell about dragons usually start with the poor creature being aggressive and stealing food. Then they end with the dragon getting stabbed, speared and killed. There are more dragon slayers in history than you can shake a stick at. Including the famous story of your St George and the dragon. Even your famous Mr Tolkien had a dragon in his stories about a Magic Ring. His dragon was called Smaug, and he successfully guarded treasure for a long while. And what happens to Smaug after all his good work? He gets killed off!

Then there's a couple of legends about dragons in the Surrey Hills. For example, there's the Dragon of Clandon. I've heard that fine creature described as having "yellow teeth with poisoned saliva". Nice way to talk about something beautiful and powerful! He ends up getting stabbed and killed by a soldier returning from the wars. All for taking a few chickens and sheep he needed for food, just to survive. Then there's the legend of Tarascus, a dragon-like creature associated with St Martha's Hill, right over there. Described as a "ferocious beast", until finally tamed by St Martha!

Tame a dragon!" exclaims Grace. " Why would anyone want to tame a dragon? Dragons are beautiful and they need to be free to go and fly where they want to in this beautiful planet."

"There must be some good dragons in the story books" I interject. "What about Zog?"

"Yes, there are some lovely stories about dragons. I just wish there were more stories about good dragons who live to do good things for the whole planet, especially lady dragons like me! So, to answer your question – yes, Grace is an unusual dragon name. But then I'm an unusual dragon."

"Do you think, Grace, that the bad reputation of dragons is sometimes justified?"

"Look, there are good humans, and not so good humans. Wouldn't you agree? I know some wonderful men, women and children who go out of their way to help others, help animals and help the planet. I have seen others who are mean to others, cruel to animals and who do things to destroy this wonderful planet on which they are guests.

Well, it's pretty much the same with dragons. Some are good, and do good things; others who can do things to hurt and upset people, and other animals. There are even dragons who are good one day, and bad the next. Sounds just like humans doesn't it?"

"Do you think, Grace, that humans have always badmouthed dragons?"

"Think about some of the ways humans use the word "Dragon," and you will have your answer." Grace responds.

"There's a range of mountains in South African called the Drakensberg. That means Dragon Mountain. They are stunning;

check them out on the web. Nearer home there are the beautiful Dragon Back Hills in Shropshire. There are beautiful Dragon Boats in the Far East. There is Dragon Tea. Very tasty! There is the famous Girl with the Dragon Tattoo. A very determined and smart young woman.

No, I think you humans can see the good things in Dragons, when you want to. But when you get nervous and afraid, you see only the bad things."

I decide to get a little bolder in my questioning. Perhaps the fact that the mist is lifting and the rain is easing gives me extra courage.

"So, Grace, you have talked quite a lot about dragons doing good things. Can you tell me of good deeds you have done?"

Grace turns slightly. Her left eye is focused, like a laser, on my head. Her huge tail moves softly, powerfully. I am sure her breath quickens a little. Have I pushed too far with my question?

"Well," says Grace. "Let me tell you a story of what happened only last week. Then you can decide if I am capable of good deeds, or not. The decision will be yours, so listen carefully!

I was here at Newlands Corner, about a week ago. Unlike today, the weather was wonderful. Amazing views across the valley.

I was clawing (that's Dragon for walking) my way along that path there, where the forest meets the open grass." Grace waves her enormous tail towards the west. "I was feeling really good, everything was calm. All of nature was in tip top form. Then after a while, I came across this big, ugly old motor car, parked right in the middle of the path.

To be honest, I could smell the car from a long way off. A nasty, oily smell. As I got closer, I could see horrible dirty smoke coming from the back of the car. I realised that, although the car was not moving, the engine was running and poison was belching from the exhaust pipe. I clawed alongside the car. All the windows were shut. There was a very large man behind the steering wheel. He was looking at his iPhone, and munching a big burger.

With one of my claws I tapped lightly on the window. I have to say that normally, when people see me, they get quite alarmed. This man however, showed almost no reaction. He simply waved me to go away, in a very rude and aggressive manner! So, I tapped on the car window again, this time with a bit more force.

He wound his window down. "What?" he shouted.

I started to explain to him that his exhaust fumes were poisoning many living things, ruining nature in this beautiful area. I said there was no need for the fumes – his car wasn't even moving!

Before I could finish, the man shouted at me. "Look. I need to run my motor to keep my air conditioner going. I don't care about your nature thing. I want to eat my burger in peace. SO, GO AWAY." (Except he didn't say "go away". He used other words I could not repeat to you.)

Then he threw his burger wrapper out of the window, shut the window in my face and went back to his iPhone.

Now Mr Interviewer" Grace said, "listen carefully.

Everybody knows Dragons can breathe out fire. But not many people know we can also breathe in fire and smoke and all kinds of nasty things. And then we use what we breathe in to produce our famous dragon fire. Which we use only when absolutely necessary, of course.

So, I went to the back of the smelly car. I used my enormous front teeth to grip the exhaust pipe. And in a very few seconds I breathed in all the nasty smoke, and all the petrol from his car.

The engine stopped with a big CLANK. The car was broken. The car door burst open. The very large man heaved himself out of the driving seat. He was very angry. Very red in the face.

"Look what you've done now. You're a vandal. You've wrecked my car. I'll get the police on you!" screamed the man.

I fixed him with my right eye. That's the one which really scares people.

"You've completely messed up my day. I've got a ticket for the big football match at Chelsea this afternoon. I am a VIP season ticket holder at the club. Thanks to you Vandal Dragon, my car is broken. I'll never make it in time." The big angry man was close to tears."

Grace turned to me. I detected a bit of a dragon smile. "It was then, Mr Interviewer," she said, "that I began to get an idea.

I looked directly at the big man who was now just a huge, messy bundle of anger, fear and disappointment. Here is what I said to him, in a very soothing tone. "This is what I can do. I will get you to your match on time. You can hop on my back and as you know, dragons can fly. So, I will fly you to the Chelsea football stadium."

"How do I know I can trust you, Vandal Dragon?" The man replied to me in a most aggressive manner.

"How else will you get to your precious football match on time?" was my reply to him.

So, the angry man huffed and puffed and climbed up on my back. He made a big fuss of it, and had to pull himself up on one of the spines on my back. But eventually he got there. He sat forward, in front of my spines, and clung on to my neck.

With a few flaps of my big wings, we were in the air.

"Hang on tight!" I called.

I adore the sound of my wings working with the air. KAWOOOSH! KAWOOOSH! KAWOOOSH!

At first, I flew very gently. Spectacular views of Leith Hill and Pitch Hill. People market shopping on Guildford High Street, jogging in the park in Reigate, sitting outside at a coffee shop in Dorking, canoeing on the River Wey, hiking by the Tillingbourne. Seeing people enjoying nature and breathing the fresh air calmed my passenger down.

Then he called out. "Time is ticking, you know. Chop, chop! I need to get to the game!"

I turned to the west, and headed for the Devil's Punchbowl.

"Oi, oi – Vandal Dragon!" He shouted "wrong direction! We need to go towards London!"

In response, I began to sing my version of an old nursery rhyme chorus, just loud enough for my passenger to hear.

"Grace goes Loop–de-Loop

Dragon goes Loop de-Li,

Grace goes Loop–de Loop,

Hang on tight while I fly."

And I flew a huge loop-de-loop in the sky.

"STOP VANDAL DRAGON. STOP!"

I did another loop, and another, then a double loop, then a spectacular triple loop.

"HELP! HELP! STOP! I'M GOING TO BE SICK! I'M GOING TO FALL!"

I stopped the aerial acrobatics and flew calmly for a minute.

"I will only stop" I told the quivering wreck on my back "if you promise never, ever again to let your foul smoke damage nature and you swear you will always respect every living thing that shares the planet with you, including dragons."

"NEVER, NEVER WILL I RESPECT YOU, VANDAL DRAGON!" he screamed at me.

We were right over the Devils Punchbowl. I made huge sweeps of my wings. I created explosive energy with the air. ZAHZOOM! ZAHZOOM! ZAHZOOM! ZAHZOOM! I flew directly upwards as far as I could. Then I completed a spectacular loop, and plunged back to earth. I stretched my long neck forward. I folded my wings. Like an arrow, we accelerated towards earth.

"HELP, HELP, WE ARE GOING TO CRASH AND DIE. I WILL NEVER WATCH CHELSEA AGAIN!" The terrified man was hanging on to my neck with all his strength. I could sense his fear.

My eyes were sharply focused on the road that bypassed the Devil's Punchbowl. As we descended at huge speed, I saw the dark opening to the Hindhead Tunnel through which the road passed. At the last possible moment, I opened my wings and held them out using them as air brakes. The noise of the wind against my wings was deafening. SKREEEEEEEECH! The strain on my dragon muscles was almost unbearable. Just in time, I stopped our descent. We swooped into the tunnel opening. We just squeezed in between the roof of the tunnel and the cars and trucks on the road below. It was dark and smelled of exhaust fumes (which I quite enjoyed inhaling!)

The angry man was flat against my back. I could just hear his cries above the roar of the traffic.

"HELP – DRAGON LADY IS GOING TO KILL US ALL."

I saw the light at the eastern end of the tunnel. We soared out and upward into the clear air.

"That was fun" I said. "Lets' do that again. I'll start with my favourite triple loop."

"NO, NO. PLEASE NO" cried the angry man. "I PROMISE TO BE GOOD. PLEASE DON'T FLY INTO THAT TUNNEL AGAIN."

"Okay" I said calmly. "Then you have to say, very clearly, after me: -

I will always respect Nature.

I will always be good to all living things.

I will get rid of my smelly car and buy a bike."

And although he struggled on every word, almost to the point of choking, the angry man made me that promise.

"One more thing" I said as we flew over the Castle in Guildford. "Hand me your phone. I need to talk to Chelsea Football Club."

Now we were flying calmly and gently over the River Wey to where it meets the Thames.

We passed over Richmond Park, and then I spied the Chelsea Football Ground in the distance.

As we got closer, we heard the roar of the crowd in the stadium. The players and the referee were already lined up on the pitch.

I swooped down, right over the top of the stands, and landed gracefully on the centre circle. I gave the ball a little kick with my claw as we touched down.

The crowd was going crazy. (I was later told that this was the first time a dragon had kicked off a football game).

The angry man was still clinging on to my neck. I could tell he wanted to get off, but was scared to move.

Then the Chelsea head coach walked out of his dugout, and came across to the centre circle.

"Hello, Grace," he said." Thanks for providing the pre-game entertainment. Our fans won't forget this for a while!"

He held up a hand to my passenger, and got him safely off my back and onto the pitch.

"Let's all look up at the electronic scoreboard," said the world-famous coaching maestro.

And there, clearly and boldly for all the fans, players and TV viewers to see: -

WELCOME TO OUR VIP SEASON TICKET HOLDER IN ROW C SEAT 5.

TODAY HE HAS COMMITTED TO:

ALWAYS RESPECT NATURE.

ALWAYS BE GOOD TO ALL LIVING THINGS.

GET RID OF HIS SMELLY CAR AND RIDE A BIKE.

LET'S ALL SUPPORT THIS.

LET'S ALL CHEER FOR DRAGON GRACE

COME ON CHELSEA!

The crowd roared, and it was time for me to leave the pitch to the players.

I flew upwards. KAWOOOSH! KAWOOOSH! KAWOOOSH! The roars and applause of the fans stayed with me and energised me as I flew back over West London. I headed to the Surrey Hills, full of confidence that my angry man would keep his word.

Does that begin to answer your question, Mr Interviewer?"

The sun was burning through now. The view was magical. I felt really good inside.

"Thank you, Grace," I said. "I have learned a lot today."

"So, it's time for me to move on. I have more dragon challenges to attend to." Grace turned and began to move away. For the first time I saw the beautiful tattoo at the base of her long neck. Around the edge of the tattoo were the words Surrey Hills SuperHero. And in the middle was a gorgeous representation of Boudicca the legendary warrior queen who confronted the Roman invaders long, long ago.

"The tattoo, Grace?" I asked.

"Well, I have been awarded the status of SuperHero of the Surrey Hills. It's a great honour and a great responsibility. And I greatly admire strong, independent, courageous women like Boudicca. So, I figured that if a human girl can have a dragon tattoo, then why can't a lady dragon have a human tattoo?"

The origin of the Loop-de-Loop chorus is a children's nursery rhyme which first appeared in 1849.

There are many legends about the Tarascus Dragon and St Martha's hill. You can check them out on the internet.

Zog is a dragon that appears in books by Julia Donaldson.

Smaug the Dragon appears in JRR Tolkien's 1937 novel The Hobbit.

All the locations mentioned in this story are well worth a visit.

THE GOLDEN THREAD OF HOPE.

ARIADNE. CRETE. THOUSANDS OF YEARS AGO.

Ariadne could feel waves of terror building up inside her, rising steadily higher, only the thoughts of her Athenian boyfriend beating back her fear. She had to succeed. She had to find her inner hero and finish the task.

The underground maze in which she stood was pitch black. The passageways smelt of death; old and stale. The roars of the Minotaur filled the air, deep intakes of breath broken by his fearsome cries. Time and time again – GRROARRRR---- PHWWWWW--- GROARRRR----PHWWWWW. They rang of hate and hunger, and death.

The Minotaur, half man, half beast, had been imprisoned in the dark, rocky maze deep below the Royal Palace in Crete longer now than anyone could remember. To survive, minotaurs needed to hunt and kill, so to keep it happy every year, young men and women were seized from Athens and shipped to the island of Crete. Sacrifices to keep the monster under control. And none have ever escaped from either the maze or the Minotaur.

Ariadne was the beautiful daughter of Minos King of Crete and she was the granddaughter of a god and a goddess.

This year one young man among the Athenian prisoners had captured Ariadne's attention. He was tall and lean with a strong face, graceful as a dancer, yet with the intense eyes of a warrior. His name was Theseus and the two had fallen in love. Ariadne was desperate to save him from certain death in the maze and with him she had devised a plan; clever, daring, and full of danger.

Ariadne alone knew all the twists and tuns of the complicated maze. She knew exactly which passages to take and which to avoid. She could lead Theseus into the maze and safely out again. But that would not be the end of the danger. The King and his guards would hunt them down. Her only option was to flee Crete with Theseus, escaping in a small boat she had waiting for them on the beach.

But first they had to get past the Minotaur and Theseus would have to confront the beast and fight for his life. She had already smuggled him a sword, now she showed him how to get into the maze. She handed him a magical golden thread. It would lead him out of the long, winding, dark, confusing, passageways and out again where Ariadne would be waiting for him. Then they would run to the beach and take to the rough seas in their boat, leaving Crete forever and finally being together. The thread of gold was their one thread of hope.

But first, Theseus had to kill the deadly Minotaur. Ariadne was a goddess, clever and brave. But in the dark, with the roars of the Minotaur pounding in her ears, she still battled with her fear. She gripped one end of the golden thread. She saw the thread shimmering like the surface of the sea on a starry night. She knew this was the reflected light of her love for Theseus. There was no other light in the passageway. She knew Theseus had reached the centre of the maze, close to the Minotaur's lair. She knew he must battle the deadly Minotaur and kill him before he could follow the golden thread of hope to safety.

Ariadne feared the Minotaur. The beast was huge, fearsome, and always hungry to kill. The beast had killed many, many times before. She knew that if Theseus won the fight and began to flee to her along the golden thread, she would feel the thread moving but the golden thread was still.

Suddenly there was a hellish scream. More powerful than the roar of the Minotaur. A single pitch, echoing on and on in the empty passageways. The scream continued for an eternity. Then nothing. Total black, horrifying, empty silence.

FRED GOODFELLOW – GUILDFORD – SATURDAY 18 JUNE, 1966.

Fred Goodfellow's life had been full of good days but this day, he decided, was by far the best. Fred was standing in St Mary's, the oldest Church in Guildford. The hymn he was singing was his favourite, by a country mile. The hymn was called "I vow to thee my country." To be honest it was one of the very few hymns Fred knew the melody and the words for.

Fred was not totally sure of the exact meaning of all the words. However, in his mind there was a powerful connection between the words of the hymn and the beautiful Surrey Hills where he lived and worked. He also felt the hymn said a lot about love. Love had brought Fred and Rosie the woman standing next to him to the Church today. The hymn perfectly summed up this perfect day for Fred and Rosie.

Fred was born just after the end of the war. He was the youngest in a family of two sisters and three brothers. His father had started work aged fourteen on a farm in the Hills. He had learned farming skills and was then called up to fight. He returned to farm work in Ash after the end of the conflict.

His mother had strong links with St. Luke's Hospital on Warren Road in Guildford where she worked as a nurse, and where all the babies she delivered had been born.

Fred loved family life. His mother's warmth and affection. His father's energy and jokes. Talking and laughing and walking and running and climbing and arguing and fighting and laughing with his brothers and sisters. Always somebody at home. Always something new to talk about. Fred liked school though more for the football, cricket and schoolyard games than the lessons in maths and history. When he looked back, Fred felt the best thing about school was Rosie. He first met her when he was fourteen. They became sweethearts and stayed sweethearts. There was no doubt, they were made for each other.

Fred left school when he was sixteen. He went straight to work for a farmer in Chilworth at the foot of the hills and forests of the Guildford Chantries. Fred was strong, agile and practical. He loved the open-air life and learned quickly. The farmer took Fred under his wing and taught him about caring for livestock and how to prepare, plant and harvest crops, fruit and vegetables. Life was good. His love continued for the open air, for the Surrey Hills and of course for Rosie.

Meanwhile his sweetheart had also left school and she had taken up nursing. She worked and studied at St. Luke's Hospital where she got to know Fred's mother well. Fred and Rosie wanted to marry. All of Fred 's sisters and brothers were now married, so much of the fun at home had gone. Rosie was an only child and longed to start a family with Fred. But the truth was, they did not have enough money to find somewhere to live.

It was Autumn 1965. The farmer and Fred were working long hours harvesting the crop. Hard, backbreaking but rewarding labour. Fred was singing the theme tune from the Beatles film HELP which he had seen with Rosie, a few weeks back. Fred was a big fan of the Beatles and loved singing their songs, although even he would admit it was unlikely he would be asked to join their band! So, after endless strangled cries of "Help", the farmer decided it was time to take a rest from the working and the singing.

Fred and the farmer sat on bales of hay, enjoying warm tea from their Thermos flasks. The farmer had been introduced to Rosie a while ago. He asked Fred how the romance was going.

"It's like this" said Fred, "we love each other very much. We would like to marry. But we don't have the money to get a place of our own."

The farmer was silent for a couple of minutes. Then he said "You know, I have a little corner of land just on the edge of my farm. It's not huge and it's overgrown. It has a small shack on it, needs a bit of work and attention, but it could be lived in. There's enough ground to grow some vegetables and fruit and to keep a pig and a couple of chickens. Maybe we could work out a way for you and Rosie to move in there?"

That was a big step along the path that led to Fred singing "I vow to thee my country" in St Mary's Church in June of the next year. Rosie, as beautiful a bride as St Mary's had seen, was by his side. Behind them, gathered in good spirits, were Rosie's mum and dad, Fred's parents, siblings and an impressive gathering of grandchildren, the farmer and his wife, and lots of friends from St Luke's Hospital. A bright, bright tomorrow dawned.

ZAK, CITY OF DARAA, SYRIA April 2012

By anybody's standards, Zak was a good lad. He was studious, did well in class. He liked maths, history and science. He made good progress in English. He excelled in computer technology. He studied the Qur'an. He said his prayers. He had visited the Mosque with his father. He helped with the kitchen and cleaning work in their two-bedroomed apartment. He had good friends from the other apartments in the block and from school.

Most people would describe Zak as "a grounded boy". He took his tasks seriously, but was not dull in personality. He was easy to talk to. His good looks helped to make him instantly likeable. His passion was football. He played football at school. He played for the local under-12's team. He practiced his skills in the local park whenever he could.

He followed football in England on television if the chance arose. His favourite team was Chelsea, although his favourite player was the England captain who played for Liverpool. Chelsea versus Liverpool matchdays were about the only stressful things in Zak's life. Apart from the exploding bombs and gunfire, of course. Not every day, or every night. But more and more frequently. Mostly in the distance, but sometimes closer. The civil war was a fact of everyday life. Like his mother and father, Zak hated it but forced himself to live with it. There was nothing they could do to change things. They just had to survive, live through it.

In many places across the world, Monday is seen as a tough day to get through. This was certainly true for Zac's family this particular

Monday. It was late in the afternoon, around five o'clock. His mother and father both worked at the University. They travelled to and from work together and Zak expected them back at any minute.

They walked through the door. They were both pale, nervous and distracted. His father asked Zak to sit down. "We have to leave," he said. "Your mother and I are both suspected of doing bad things by the Government. We have to go."

"What...like when ......where? I have a match tomorrow. It's an important one."

In the end there was not much else to say. There was too much to prepare and no time to discuss it. Their freedom was threatened and their lives were at risk. They had no choice; they had to flee. There was no other option but to attempt a dangerous trek to England where they had relatives.

Zak's life and that of his parents changed beyond all recognition. None of the change was for the good. The journey was a long horror story. Exhaustion, fear, boredom, discomfort, hunger, thirst. All dignity gone. Fear at every frontier. Cash passing from hand to hand. Backs and trunks of cars. Backs of lorries. Stinking holds of boats. Hard mattresses on hard floors. Hard, cold, men and women. The bond between Zak and his parents strengthened. Their bond was the rope that guided them, pulled them to England.

The reality of England did not correspond with the picture that Zac had in his mind. Zac had expected quaint villages and huge football stadiums. He found the grey forbidding concrete buildings in which they were housed. Endless questions from the authorities. Constant moving from one uninspiring area to another. Heavy skies and cold winds. People and landscape often unwelcoming.

After four long years, a welcome degree of stability entered their lives. They were found permanent accommodation in the outskirts of London. Zac could continue his education in the local school. His mother found work as a domestic cleaner. His father worked nights, cleaning the windows of local stores.

Zac was desperate for acceptance, eager for friends. This was not easy. He was a Syrian. He was an outsider. Zac's drive for inclusion drove him to run with a local gang of teenagers. His parents saw this and pleaded with him to find other friends. The bond loosened.

Zac got into petty crime. He became known to the police. He ended up before the Magistrate. Zac had reached another turning point in his life. The Magistrate required him to spend a six-month period in a learning environment in the English countryside. He was to study all elements of English nature and work to integrate into a new way of life.

And that's how Zac ended up in the Surrey Hills, in a building he shared with other recent young immigrants also struggling to adapt. The building was near the home that Fred and Rosie had made for themselves at the foot of the wooded, hilly Chantries.

ARIADNE. THE EASTERN MEDITERRANEAN.

The silence froze Ariadne. The silence in the maze. The stillness of the golden thread she held. Was all lost? Then, a faint tremor in the string. The gold glinted just a little. More movement. A slight pulling. At last, the faint sound of feet shuffling, moving on the rock floor. And then Theseus, bloody, cut, bruised, beaten but alive. Ariadne embraced him. Then immediately, she heard the sounds of the King's guards calling to each other, calling to their hounds, searching for them.

The hounds could smell the blood of the Minotaur on Theseus and gave chase, leading the guards who were close behind. Theseus and Ariadne ran for their lives, lungs aching, legs failing and then they saw the beach, the waves crashing against their waiting boat.

They plunged into the surf and the boatman, fear in his eyes, quickly pulled Ariadne on board. Theseus, now even more exhausted, almost drowned but the boatman and Ariadne just managed to pull him on board away from the powerful current. The hounds snapped at his legs but the boatman managed to beat them back with an oar. The sails were quickly raised and they were finally free from Crete.

They set course for Naxos, an island between Crete and the mainland of Greece. Onboard the small boat, Theseus and Ariadne slept a disturbed sleep, full of monsters and dark passageways, crashing waves and howling wind. They arrived exhausted. Hunger and thirst wracked their bodies. Theseus' wounds cried out for attention.

They rested for three nights and two days on Naxos, slowly recovering from the horrors they had experienced. Ariadne regained her health and energy quickly. She saw Theseus remained scarred by his terrible struggle with the Minotaur. Then, when Ariadne awoke on the third morning, there was no Theseus by her side.

She ran to where their boatman slept. She aroused him. "Have you seen Theseus?"

The boatman's eyes betrayed his knowledge. "Madam, he left in the night. He took the boat. I don't know where he was going."

Ariadne's grief ran to days, then weeks. Why, oh why, had her Theseus deserted her? Ariadne was a goddess, and in the end, she harnessed her powers to heal the scars of Theseus' desertion. Her powers banished her despair, and in its place created two immensely strong resolutions. For the rest of her stay on the planet, she would lead a full and worthwhile life. And she would seek others who were in dark places and needed to be led out into the light. She would use her ability to create golden threads of hope wherever she could.

THE RISE AND DECLINE OF FARMER GOODFELLOW.
GUILDFORD CHANTRIES. 1966 ONWARDS

Fred and Rosie worked hard to build a good life together. Fred took on increasing responsibility with the farmer. He oversaw virtually all activities on the farm. He gained knowledge through practical experience, achieved respect in the community and became known locally as Farmer Goodfellow.

Rosie was equally respected at St Luke's Hospital. Through practical experience and the courses she took, she became increasingly important to the functioning of St Luke's.

Outside of work, they were absorbed by two huge interests. The first was their home. When the farmer he worked for had told Fred that the shack and garden "needed a little care" he had made the biggest understatement of all time.

Over the years, they fixed the roof, re-did the floor, installed a proper bathroom and kitchen, painted everything inside and out and found furniture and fabric that made their house warm and cosy. Then they turned their attention to the small plot of land surrounding the shack. Clearing the overgrown hedges, saplings and brambles was a full autumn's work. They could then set out the vegetable garden, plant apple and pear trees and create shelters for their chickens and the pig.

Gradually and increasingly, the house became a home and the land provided a significant amount of their daily food needs. Their second huge interest was walking in the Surrey Hills. This was their Sunday morning treat. After a hard working week and a Saturday focused on home and garden, roaming the Hills provided new energy, new refreshment. All weathers, all seasons inspired them. As Fred would often say as they climbed Leith Hill, "Just breathing in this air makes me feel better and stronger inside."

Their one big disappointment was the absence of children. It just did not happen for them. Farmer Goodfellow and Rosie handled this as they handled all of life's challenges. They accepted it and put extra effort into work, home, hiking and roaming, and keeping close to nephews, nieces and their parents. Life was good, if not complete.

In retrospect, 1991 was the year when things started to change. St Luke's Hospital closed and Rosie lost her job. She continued to work part time, caring for people in their homes, but she missed the life she had enjoyed at the Hospital. Over the next years, they lost both sets of parents. Nephews and nieces moved away in increasing numbers, following work and education opportunities, starting families of their own. The family became much smaller.

To keep their spirits up, Fred and Rosie focused on their Golden Wedding anniversary; in 2016, they would be celebrating fifty years of marriage. They planned a great celebration. But just a year before Fred's sixty-fifth birthday, another bombshell. The farm on which he had worked all his life was sold. Much of the land was to be used for housing development. The plot opposite Fred and Rosie's was donated as a "Rural Centre for Learning and Integration." "Whatever that means!" said Rosie.

The silver lining was that Fred and Rosie could stay on their small plot of land for as long as they lived. Although Fred's full-time job was over, there would be occasional part-time work for him on the land as the new development progressed.

"Oh well," said Fred. "We've got each other, we've got our home, we've got the Hills, and we've got our anniversary to look forward to."

The Rural Centre was the first piece of construction. It was a large wooden building, nicely designed to fit in with the landscape. Young men and women began arriving. As far as the Goodfellows could see, individuals stayed at the Centre for between three and six months. Fred knew there were classrooms in the building. He met an acquaintance one day, a specialist in tree care and maintenance. They chatted. His old friend told him he was delivering lectures at the Centre, helping the young people become familiar with the Surrey countryside.

At other times, Fred saw groups heading off on hikes led by a guide. In the evenings, groups often sat out in the open around firepits. There was fun and laughter. Fred suspected campfire stories were being told.

Fred and Rosie had little contact with the young people in the Centre. They occasionally offered a "good morning," or waved a hand, but the young people seemed uninterested, withdrawn. Fred suspected that many of them did not speak English.

Keeping their land productive, walking in the Hills and preparing for their Golden Anniversary filled their time. And then, just two years before the anniversary date, Rosie was diagnosed with a terminal illness. Rosie fought the illness with courage and calm. Fred was devastated. Inside he was beaten, almost defeated. Rosie received care beyond words from the Royal Surrey County Hospital. To the last, she remained positive and calm.

Rosie died just two weeks before the Golden anniversary. Fred Goodfellow's grief was black, unending, cruel, suffocating. He aged rapidly. He stooped. He began to limp. He lost all interest in the things around him. The land became totally overgrown. The chickens ran wild. The pig uncared for. Hikes in the Hills no longer interested him. He became rude and aggressive to others. He shouted and screamed at things which upset him. He became annoyed by the young people in the Centre. He was sure that they were laughing at him. Imitating his stoop and his limp.

More and more he stayed inside. His home became dirty, damp, uncared for. He no longer made proper food. One year after Rosie's death, Fred was a sad hermit. He knew he was close to the end of his life. He lay on his filthy bed and didn't care any more.

ZAC – RURAL CENTRE FOR LEARNING

From the start, Zac felt at ease in the Rural Centre. The accommodation was basic, clean and simple. The food was regular, tasty and wholesome. All the staff were friendly and easy to talk to. Zac particularly liked the people who came in to deliver lectures, to lead them on hikes, to tell the stories and legends of the land in which they lived.

Young men and women from many backgrounds arrived and worked and studied in the Centre. They came from families who had originated in Iraq, Libya, Tunisia, Afghanistan, Palestine and Syria like Zac. The common language was English. Some like Zac spoke fluently, and understood completely. For others, English was work in process. Because everyone was "an outsider", nobody was an outsider. The one thing in common was the need to integrate into the English way of life. That's what they were there for.

Zac was generally popular. He knew pretty much all the people in the Centre. He went out of his way to help others with their projects, their computer skills and with their English. He became close friends with a young woman whose family originated in Afghanistan. Aisha like Zac had experienced difficulty in integrating in England. Aisha had been badly injured in a bomb attack in Kabul. This left her with a pronounced limp and she felt mocked and bullied in her English school because of this. She had run away from home, slept rough and eventually stole food to survive. This was her path to the Rural Centre.

Zac learned. He absorbed the lectures on English country life, agriculture, the care of livestock. They visited Merrist Wood, a local College specialising in many kinds of careers "in the natural world." They toured the Horticultural Gardens at Wisley and Zak fell in love with their beauty. At Painshill Park, Tangley Manor, Farnham Castle and Loseley, Zac began an on-going love affair with the English landscape.

Zac became "King of the Hill" at the Centre; he was always at the front of the hiking parties, especially on the climbs. When he first arrived in England, he missed the dry climate of Syria. Now, as he stormed up Box Hill and breathed in the cool damp air, it was almost intoxicating. The fresh oxygen ignited his inner hero. He had found a new home.

Parties round the camp fire in the evenings were by far Zac's favourite part of life at the Centre. Sitting on the ground with the smell of the forest and the moon and stars above, the sense of belonging was overpowering. The young people would tell stories to each other. Sometimes storytellers from the Surrey area would visit and recount legends of Silent Pool, and St Martha's Hill as well as daring deeds from long ago. Zac began to understand his environment.

About half way through his stay, Zac was returning from a walk in the forest. Aisha, limping a little from the effort of the hike, was with him. They saw the small cottage of the old man who lived opposite. Neither Zac or Aisha knew much about him; some of the other students thought him rude and aggressive, said his name was Farmer Goodfellow.

As they passed the cottage, the door opened. The old man, dishevelled, thin, worn, took a couple of painful steps down the garden path. He looked towards Aisha and then toward Zak. Painfully he raised one arm. In a manner neither aggressive, nor friendly, he beckoned them over.

FARMER GOODFELLOWS DREAM.

As he slipped towards sleep, Fred was convinced this was his last night. He felt no fear, or regret. The good times of his life were over, there was only misery left. Then, suddenly, he was awake, senses fully alive. The night outside was still dark. The room was bright. Across the small room stood a beautiful woman. Eyes and face bright. A faint smile on her lips. A shining golden thread in her hand.

"I am Ariadne," she said. "I am a goddess. Let's for the moment call me the goddess of communication. I once experienced deep grief, total blackness in my life. I had to learn to deal with it. That took a long, long time. But when I triumphed over the dark, I vowed to seek others in desperate times and help them find a way out of it. That's all you need to know about me. The reason I am here is to listen to and understand your story. Will you tell it to me?"

The goddess was warm, her presence both enticing and energising. In recent times, Fred would have brushed aside invitations to tell his history. Now, he wanted to talk. He recounted his life from his earliest memories, right up to falling asleep this night. He recounted the highs and the lows. The good times and the bad.

"So, you see Goddess Ariadne" he said at last, "I am old, tired, run down and miserable. I am no longer strong. I can't even tend my plot of land anymore. All my life I have worked to produce food for others. Now I can't even produce food for myself. I hear there are all kinds of new farming methods. I am so out of date. I can't keep up. Farmer Goodfellow is a Dinosaur! Nobody loves me. Nobody likes me. I am totally alone. The planet doesn't need me anymore. I must go away in peace."

Ariadne let him tell his story. At the end, she smiled warmly, said nothing for a while. "I suppose" she finally said, "you think this is the first time I have heard a story like yours? I suppose," she continued "you think that everybody else has a life that is all good, no problems, no challenges. Just a bed of roses! But, so that you don't think I am tough and cruel - I like your story! I like it because it is true. At least most of it is true. But you did tell me two whopping ugly, nasty lies. Or perhaps I should say, you told yourself two shameful, shocking lies. And lying to yourself, Fred, is almost worse than lying to others. Liar, liar, pants on fire! And who gets burned first when your pants are on fire?"

Fred was reduced to a shivering wreck. He gurgled and burbled a bit.

"So, you don't need to ask me what your "woe is me – I feel sorry for myself" lies are. You don't need to ask because I'm going to tell you anyway. So, pin back your ears, Fred Goodfellow, and listen well.

First the planet does need you and you must respect that, and repay the hospitality the planet has given you all these years. You have huge experience of the land on which you live. For over fifty years you have farmed this land. You have grown crops, you have tended livestock. You know about nature, about the seasons, about the soil, about wild animals and about the importance of plants and trees and insects, all vital to this piece of land, vital to this planet. It is your duty to share this knowledge with young people. Help them understand what you know. Help them treat the land well and avoid some of the mistakes previous generations made. There is a group of young people right over the road from you..."

Fred began to say he didn't like the young people, but Ariadne cut him right off. "I don't care much about what you like and what you don't like. I care about what you need to do. These young people have a huge thirst for knowledge about the countryside, about the Surrey Hills. You can help provide that knowledge. You should do that. You told me about twenty times in your story of your life how much you loved Rosie. So, Rosie was a nurse. She cared for people. If you want to respect the memory of Rosie, you should care for people too. So, get yourself over to the Rural Centre and start caring about some of those kids."

Fred was so far on the defensive now, he could only try to deflect the torrent of common sense launched at him by Ariadne. "You said there were two lies" he said, without much conviction.

Ariadne was on super form. "Ah yes – the bit about not being able to keep up with the latest farming trends. Being a Dinosaur. Well Fred – it's not that you can't keep up, it's that you won't keep up! You enjoy being a Dinosaur!"

Ariadne began to play with the golden thread. "You see this golden thread. It connected me to Theseus. It gave Theseus the courage to kill the Minotaur and the knowledge to get out of the maze. It prevented me from running off on my own. As long as I was connected to Theseus by the thread, I had hope. You want to know what today's golden thread is called?"

Fred remained silent.

"It's called the internet, Fred. The internet can connect you to just about any farmer in the world. To farmers' groups, to experts in farming. Get on the web, and you'll find how today's methods can help you manage even your small plot of land. Even though you say you are old and doddery -the third lie which luckily for you we won't talk about – you'll be producing enough to live on in no time."

"I hate the internet, I don't understand it. It makes me go all wobbly at the knees!"

"So, when you go and meet the young people at the Centre, make sure you talk to one called Zac. He is the super whiz bang techno king of all time. I am pretty sure that if you help him and his pals, he will help you set up on the web. You might even get to like the web. Who knows, you two might even get to like each other!"

The golden thread glistened and shone brightly. Then Ariadne was gone. The room was dark again. Fred fell almost immediately into a deep untroubled sleep.

THE DAWN AFTER THE DREAM

Fred Goodfellow awoke the next morning. All dark thoughts had gone. His mind was now crystal clear and focused. It was simple. For the rest of his life he had to behave in a way that showed respect to the memory of Rosie. And he had a lot of ground to make up! He didn't care whether the encounter with Ariadne was real or a dream. He did care that the words she has spoken were true. Her words had energised him. He wanted to act, that was clear. He saw that he needed to relate to others as Ariadne had related to him. Straightforward. Tell it as it is. Positive. On the front foot.

Whether he realised he had fallen a little bit in love with Ariadne was unclear. Her charm had mesmerised him, weakened his stubbornness, made her tough words more acceptable. For the first time in a long time, Fred got up early. He had a single egg, and some bread left in the pantry. He made himself a proper breakfast. He ate it at the table.

Then he started the Herculean task of cleaning the house. He worked steadily, humming some of his favourite Beatles tunes to keep the rhythm of his work going. A little before midday, he glanced through his very dirty front window. Two of the young people from the Rural Centre were passing. "Strike while the iron's hot!" thought Fred. He stopped cleaning, took a few steps down his path. This caught their attention. He beckoned them to come over.

This first meeting between Fred, Aisha and Zac had an edgy, uncomfortable start. Aisha and Zac were reluctant to walk up the path. Fred was reluctant to show weakness by going over to them. Eventually a compromise meeting happened in the middle of the path. "I should tell you right away that I don't much like you young people," Fred started. He was clearly following Ariadne's directness and honesty but he couldn't as easily replicate her charm!

Aisha turned to go away, stung by Fred's rudeness. Zac, who had learned the value of curiosity above judgment, kept the meeting alive. "Now why's that sir?" he asked. "What is it about us that you don't like?"

"You make fun of me", said Fred. "I'm old and have a gammy leg. I've seen one of you mimic my way of walking. I suppose you all think that's funny? And most of you don't talk English!"

Zac gave Aisha's hand a little squeeze. "Well sir," he said, "I understand what you are saying. It's good that you've told us but I think we can deal with your concerns. The young person who has the injured leg is Aisha, this young woman by my side. Her leg was badly damaged in a bomb blast during a war in the country where she was born. She has had to work incredibly hard to walk at all. But walk everyday she does, and every day she walks better. So please do not see her way of walking as mocking or mimicking you. Please see it as a mark of determination by this beautiful young woman. A determination to fully explore the stunning Surrey Hills in spite of the difficulties put in her way."

Fred's felt ashamed. He clearly had much work to do before he achieved the ability to talk to others as Ariadne had talked to him.

"And while we talk about Aisha, I should get you up to date on languages. Everyone at the Centre speaks some English plus the language they grew up with. Aisha speaks four languages. Her English is way better than mine and she also speaks Dari Persian, Pasto and a little Russian. So, I'm pretty sure that between us all, we can find a way to communicate well."

Fred was determined to follow the Ariadne example and stay as positive as possible. "I may have been a bit hasty in the way I was looking at things," he said. "but do you know a boy called Zac? I really want to talk to him."

Before Aisha could give the game away, Zac replied. "What do you want to talk to Zac about?"

"Well, it's like this", said Fred. "I have a deal to propose. If this Zac helps me with a tecno-thingy problem that I have, I can help Zac by showing him the Surrey Hills, telling him about the history of the beautiful places and letting him know everything I have learned in over fifty years of farming."

To Zac's surprise, Aisha jumped in with a response. "Ah, Farmer Goodfellow. We don't work like that. We don't do deals. At the Centre, we work as a team. We all agree to do something or we don't do it. We won't do things for you just because you do things for us. If you have something that you need help on and we can help, we'll do it. If you can do something for us that we all like, we'll gladly accept."

Fred felt the initiative slipping away. The talk with Ariadne's felt a long time back now. He mumbled a few words. "So, err, so um, what happens err next?" he managed.

"We're having a campfire tonight" said Zac. "The whole team will be there. Come on over and join us. You might enjoy it! You can tell everyone your story and tell us where you need help and explain your ideas of how you can share your experience with the team. We'll see what happens."

That afternoon was the most nervous time in Fred's life. Time after time, he rehearsed in his mind how he would recount his story and how he would explain the experiences he had gained and could share with the young people. He decided it would be a good idea to have a bath and smarten himself up.

It was a relief when dusk came and Fred saw the campfire starting to burn. He walked over to the Centre as calmly as he could. Aisha greeted him and led him over to the gang around the fire.

"Look, it's all super-informal" she said." I'm not going to introduce you to everyone individually. You'll just forget their names. Just chill and settle in, then in about half an hour, I'll ask you to talk to us."

Aisha found Fred a seat on a log between brothers who had arrived at the Centre just last week. There was a great atmosphere around the fire and Fred sensed there were many stories and tales being told, maybe even a few jokes. The brothers were keen to tell Fred about their adventures. He tried to listen carefully but he was distracted by his own nervousness. In his mind he kept rehearsing the things he wanted to say.

Fred saw the young man he had talked with earlier arrive and sit opposite him across the fire. A young woman with a guitar then joined and started strumming tunes. The magic of the Hills was in the air. Fred breathed deeply and began to relax.

Aisha stood up. "Hi everyone, welcome to another amazing Rural Centre campfire. I'd like to introduce you all to a guest. Welcome Farmer Fred Goodfellow who has lived in the Hills right opposite where we are now for many, many years. Aisha made a big gesture toward Fred who stood up to scattered applause. Fred is here to tell us about his life and about a few things we might decide to do together.

So, Fred, with increasing confidence, told the story of a young boy growing up in the Surrey Hills. He talked about his family and how he became involved in farming. He made sure to keep the tone as interesting and positive as he could. When he got to the part about taking Rosie to a film with the Beatles, someone called out-

"Yeah, we like the Beatles. Give us a song Farmer Fred!"

Fred sensed his moment. "Will you help me a bit?" he called to the guitar player. She came around and joined him. He said a few quiet words in her ear. Then together they sang the song "With a Little Help from My Friends." An all-time favourite of Rosie and Fred. The group joined the chorus with huge enthusiasm. They demanded two encores. Fred's timing, if not his singing, was immaculate. He held the young people in the palm of his hand.

After the song, he finished his life story. He talked about the death of Rosie and the way his whole life had changed in an honest and straightforward way. He didn't whine or complain, he just told it the way it was. He explained to his audience that he needed help and information from the global farming community and was honest that he was completely lost in the techno world. (Although he didn't tell the group that it was the Goddess Ariadne who had explained the power of the internet. He thought for the moment that talking about his conversations with a goddess might be a step too far).

He explained his knowledge of the Surrey Hills with great care. He didn't want to appear as a know-all. Just as a possible guide to the group to help them find their own "inner heroes" in the Hills. He finished to warm applause and a few shouts for more Beatles songs. Then Aisha was on her feet.

"Thank you, Farmer Fred," she said. "I'd like to ask our team two questions. First, are we able to help Fred with his internet connections and get him linked up to the global farming world? Second, would we like Fred to help us understand the history of nature and agriculture in these beautiful Hills?"

There was a pause. Then one of the young men next to Fred jumped up. "Guys, this is a no brainer. It's yes to both questions. Right team?" The shouts and applause indicated full approval.

"Not so fast," said Aisha "Do we know anyone who has the tech skills to make sure Fred gets linked into the global web and then explain to him how to use it and connect with other farmers across the planet?"

"Easy". said the other brother "Even I know that and I've only been here a few weeks. Zac's the man!" He pointed directly across the campfire to the quiet smiling face of the young man Fred had talked with that morning. The whole group was in on the deception and laughed at the practical joke that had been played. Fred saw the funny side of what had happened. He was now part of a group. He could laugh too!

TWO YEARS AFTER THE CAMPFIRE

Farmer Fred Goodfellow is leading a good life. He is content, fulfilled, busy. With the efforts of Zac and the rest of the team, Fred is connected to the internet and surprisingly skilled at using it. Fred still calls it his "golden thread of hope". Through the web, he has gathered plenty of good advice on farming a small piece of land and now produces most of his own food. He is able to do this without much of the backbreaking labour of the past. Fred is a highly respected member of the Global What's App group "More from Less."

Fred is an institution at the Rural Centre. Hundreds of young people who have passed through the Centre have benefited from his experience and knowledge of the Surrey Hills. Fred's vigorous group hikes up Box Hill are part of the folklore of the Centre. One of Fred's most treasured possessions is a hiking sweatshirt given to him by a particularly energetic group from the Centre.

On the front, a picture of Fred's "Surrey Hills SuperHero" award. On the back, Fred's favourite saying. He was known for these words; they were his trademark. "Walk the Surrey Hills. Breathe in the magic. Find your inner hero."

Zac left the Rural Centre a profoundly changed young man. He had breathed in the magic deeply. He had found his inner hero. He was at home. He belonged. He studied at Merrist Wood for a year, then got an apprentice's job at Wisley Gardens. He remains in contact with Fred and occasionally helps him with IT problems.

Aisha also benefited from the magic of the Hills. She has started a Nursing course. She is an exemplary student. She lives with Zac. The two brothers who helped Fred sell his ideas at the campfire have become outstanding athletes. The younger brother is a leading English cross-country cyclist. The older one works at the Surrey Sports Park and plays rugby for the Harlequins. He is tipped as a future England captain. They both started their interest in sport at the Centre.

Ariadne continues to look for people who she can lead from the dark to the light. She still uses her golden thread as a way of explaining the importance of communicating with and relating to others.

It is said she has found no better place in all the planet than the Surrey Hills to "Breathe in the magic and find your inner hero."

Ariadne, the two brothers, Aisha and Zac along with Farmer Fred Goodfellow are now all Surrey Hills SuperHeroes.

CATS CAN BE SUPERHEROES TOO

This Surrey Hills SuperHero story has cats at its centre. It talks about the importance of staying on course when good plans look like they are failing. The story draws on the legend of the Surrey Panther. The Panther is a formidable sometimes menacing very large cat which has been sighted and written about on many, many occasions in the Surrey Hills Area.

The story features characters we have met in previous stories. Amy Elizabeth, who we met in The Green Man SuperHero story, has a prominent role in leading the SuperHero team out of despair when plans seem to be going wrong. Vesta, Goddess of Fire, Ariadne, and of course the Green Man himself, all re-appear.

GUIILDFORD TOWN CENTRE – HALLOWEEN – SATURDAY NIGHT

These two were not really bad people. They were young; he was twenty, and she was nineteen. They were energetic. And they certainly pushed against the rules from time to time. They had been out in Guildford Town Centre celebrating. Kyle because he had just been accepted into Merrist Wood college to study

Horticulture and Landscaping, Daksha because she simply liked celebrating...she also liked Kyle. They had shared a pizza, had a few drinks in a pub, then carried on partying in a night club.

Now they were in the gardens of Guildford Castle. The gardens may have been officially closed, and they shouldn't have been there, but that was a big part of the fun. Always pushing the rules, even just a little. They had found a wall they could clamber over, and were larking about in the beautiful gardens, running down the zig-zag paths, and energised on lungsful of crisp, clear night air. Naturally creative, they danced like Romeo and Juliet. They sang Adele songs. They stared up at the starry night sky pretending to navigate like ancient sailors. Against the eery backdrop of the magnificent castle ruins they became Viking invaders, Norman conquerors, Saxon serfs, Tudor monarchs, Victorian explorers, Bonny and Clyde, and Ghostbusters.

"Hide and seek," cried Kyle. "Thirty seconds to hide starting from now and I bet I can find you well before dawn!"

Daksha ran across the lawns, away from the Castle Mound. She was sure she could reach the statue of Alice through the Looking Glass in less than the thirty seconds. There were trees and bushes though along the path and the light was dimmer. She became less sure of the route she knew so well in the daytime. Then she saw the statue of Alice, a little light shimmering off the Looking Glass. She sprinted to the statue and crouched behind it, well concealed.

She heard Kyle's voice coming out of the dark. "Coming, ready or not!"

Then silence. No approaching footsteps. No more shouts from Kyle. She guessed he was exploring another route. Perhaps towards the Bowling Green?

She felt just for a moment that in all the world there was just her and Alice. Would she, like Alice, fall through a looking glass into a crazy world? The thought was unsettling. She moved a little so she could look out from behind the statue. Still no sign of Kyle.

Everything was quiet. Then, very faintly, a low guttural noise. A noise somewhere between living and mechanical. Perhaps a huge engine starting to work, way in the distance. Or something like breathing in and out? Brrrrr...

All the fun of the evening suddenly drained from Daksha. Was this a cruel trick being played on her by Kyle?

She stayed behind Alice's statue. It became a refuge. She looked and looked and listened in vain for Kyle. Nothing.

Then, away to her right, by a bench a large black shape. Moving effortlessly slowly along the path.

Daksha screamed and ran. The huge energy of fear inside her. Driving her muscles, her voice, her determination.

Daksha ran back along the path towards the Castle. She only looked forward. She didn't dare check if she was being followed.

Suddenly, she saw Kyle. Standing on the path, his attention glued to his iPhone. Totally relaxed and unconcerned.

In a rush, she ran to him and flung her arms around him. The iPhone fell to the ground.

Daksha was in a panic, desperate to tell Kyle all she had heard and seen.

Kyle was still in party mood. "Well, you are not much good at Hide and Seek", he said. "But look at this fine carriage I've found for us, half hidden in the bushes."

He turned and pointed to a small two-seater truck with an open back. The kind that park keepers use to collect garden waste. "I was just checking on my phone to see how I could get it to start. Luckily, I found out before you knocked my phone to the ground.

Step in madam for a magical mystery tour of the Castle Grounds."

"Kyle. I really think we should leave. I need to talk to you. Let's get out of here."

"Well my lady", said Kyle, still full of fun, and totally unaware of the fright Daksha had had "If you won't come, I'll have to go alone."

The thought of being alone in the park decided it. Daksha climbed with trepidation into the Parks vehicle. Kyle manged to get the electric cart going. He was singing at the top of his voice. Beautiful Ghosts by Taylor Swift, from the musical Cats. He'd heard it that evening in the pub. Though in truth, he was singing in a raucous, non-Taylor Swift way. Jumbling up the words, singing far too loudly.

"Please, keep the noise down and concentrate on what you are doing," pleaded Daksha.

To Daksha's surprise and relief, Kyle stopped his singing, and succeeded in getting the truck out on to the path.

The silence of the night returned, then suddenly out of the dark, Daksha heard the low guttural noise again. The almost mechanical breathing in and out. Brrrrr…..

This time Kyle heard too. He fumbled for the vehicle's headlights and switched them on.

No more than two metres in front of the vehicle was a huge, black creature. Just sitting there. Making that low rasping noise. Brrrrr…..…Breathing out and breathing in. Almost purring. Brrrrrrr…………..

The headlights reflected sharply in the creature's emerald green eyes, its glossy black coat, its perfectly angled face. The creature was seated neatly, its long tail wrapped around its front legs, its pointed ears high and alert on its head.

A cat! A huge domestic cat? Over a metre high. Or the legendary Surrey Puma?

Yet there was no sense of malice. The creature conveyed calm, understanding, intelligence, and a sense of being one with nature, a sense of belonging. Kyle and Daksha were in this creature's world now.

Kyle and Daksha were compelled to look straight into the creature's eyes They read the message. No need for growls or threat. The contained power of the creature, its composure, said it all.

"Time to grow up. Time to go home and relax. Time for calm before damage is done".

Kyle switched off the vehicle lights. He and Daksha got out of the vehicle. Slowly, trying to show respect, they made their way past the creature, still sitting calmly, now purring more gently. Hand in hand they made their way out of the park, over the wall and home.

A BIG BORING SHISH MEETING.

From time to time, the Surrey Hills Superheroes get together to chat things over. The secret code SHISH is passed around, a location and time is given and all those who can, attend. This meeting was high up on Pitch hill, and The Green Man, Vesta Goddess of Fire, Ariadne, and their invited guest Amy Elizabeth are present.

To be honest, Amy Elizabeth regarded meetings in the same way as she regarded Church sermons (and she had experienced few of these.) The shorter, the better summed up her view.

The gods, goddesses, and humans with magical powers like the Green Man all loved to gossip. They loved to go on and on about who said what to whom, who went where, who was angry with whom, who was upset; all this plus endless debate on the general state of the planet. They could gossip for hours, sometimes for days. It was their way of communicating things to each other. Usually in a good-natured way. Amy Elizabeth didn't mind a bit of gossip. But about five minutes was enough for her. Then she liked to get on with doing things that mattered.

This time was different. All the SuperHeroes were in a bad mood. Their gossip was miserable, negative, dispiriting. It gave Amy Elizabeth a big headache. It drained all her energy. It made her put her hands over her ears.

"You know what," said Ariadne, "I think I'm a nice person, I want to be seen as caring. I am as committed as a goddess can be to helping people out of dark places. Getting them back on their feet when they've been through tough times.

But I see so many people today who are not happy. And guess what the problem is. They have so much, they don't enjoy the things they have. Take the Surrey Hills for example, a place of beauty that I love to visit. I see some people who have big flashy cars, big luxurious houses, always flying here and there on holiday, always buying stuff from luxury stores, always hunting down the latest restaurant or coffee shop, always taking photos of what they're doing and sending them off to friends. They are so busy doing and buying stuff, that they don't have time to be happy. They just don't pause, breathe deeply, look up, and enjoy the wonderful natural world around them. They would be so much happier if they took a little time to enjoy the beauty of the Hills. I really want to help people. But I can't help them all. I'm wearing myself out!"

"You think you've got it bad," said Vesta Goddess of Fire. "I've worked and worked to get people to use fire properly, sensibly. You think it would be obvious. But still, lighted cigarettes thrown here and there out of car windows, into rubbish cans. Barbecues on the beach, barbecues in the forests of the Surrey Hills. No sense and no care. All manner of fires. Firemen rushing here and there all times of the night and day. And I haven't even started to talk about people who want to start a war. All the huge fires and misery that causes.

Like you Ariadne, I'm tired. I was talking to my good friend Eleanor the Invisible, just the other day. I said to her, "Eleanor my love, I'm up to here with it all. Much more of this and I'm packing up. And you know, Eleanor thinks just the same way"

"You guys have it easy, compared to what I have to put up with" mumbled the Green Man, in a very dull tone. "Amy Elizabeth and I put together this big plan to stop people throwing litter in the beautiful forests of the Surrey Hills. It helped, but still some slubberdegullions throw litter around. I don't know if I can go on……….".

Amy Elizabeth was at the edge of her very limited patience. "Please stop all this complaining and moaning. We've got a job to do here. We've got our planet to look after. You can't give up now. If we lose your magical powers and all your wisdom, we'll all be doomed. This is a fight worth fighting, we should never give up!"

"It's all very well saying that young lady, but we are all tired", said Vesta. "You humans have done a lot of damage to the planet. You really can't expect us to keep on helping you forever and ever….'

"So, let's talk about forever and ever" Amy Elizabeth cut in. "The planet has been around for over four billion years. Some of you SuperHeroes have been around pretty much from the start. Helping develop the planet. Helping living things develop".

She looked straight at the Green Man, who was in a particular grump. "You yourself, Mr Green Man, told me how tough it was to develop plants when they first emerged from the seas. But you kept at it and worked with nature. Now, look at these magnificent trees around us. And you told me the trees can get diseases. Do you give up when they get sick? No, you keep at it, finding ways to fight disease."

Amy Elizabeth sensed she had got the attention of the SuperHeroes. She made the most of her opportunity.

"Mankind only arrived on the planet five million years ago. By your standards, that's practically yesterday! And we've learned, we've changed as the planet has changed, and we've adapted. Sure, we've done some bad things. We've also done a lot of good.

Then some things started to happen, only about two or three hundred years ago. Big things, that changed everything. We learned how to take better care of our health. So we live longer and there are a lot more of us. And we learned how to make lots and lots of stuff. The kind of things you were talking about, Ariadne.

Cars, and aeroplanes, and new clothes, and all kinds of kit for our homes. Life changed in a big, big way."

Amy Elizabeth paused. Looked at each of the SuperHeroes straight into their eyes.

"We are learning to deal with these things. It's not easy. But there are good signs. People of my age, my friends, the people I go to school with, are the first generation to face all of these huge issues. But we all really care for the planet in a big, big way. All of us. We care about pollution and taking care of the environment. We care about the way we live. We care about not having terrible wars. If you SuperHeroes give up now, we are all lost. So please, please stay with us. Give us the time to learn, and adapt, and change. SuperHeroes don't walk off at the first sign of trouble. They stay the course. They fight through and win!"

Amy Elizabeth's words, and the energy with which she delivered them, had a big impact. At the very least, the complaining and moaning stopped. Then, after a long pause, the Green Man lifted his head slowly. He looked at the other SuperHeroes, then at Amy Elizabeth.

"Well, "he said, "If we are to keep on doing the good work, we need to change something. We need to have a new approach, a new plan, to help us get going again."

Again, a long silence, the SuperHeroes deep in thought.

Then "Cats," in a clear calm voice, from Ariadne.

"Nice one, Ariadne. Cats," said the Green Man, now at last in a positive tone.

"Yes. Yes, I get it, of course. Cats. Good call," said Vesta.

Amy Elizabeth didn't get it at all. She had made the speech of her life, on a subject of mega-importance, to three Surrey Hills SuperHeroes, and all she got in return was "Cats!"

"I don't get it, "said Amy Elizabeth, a hint of accusation in her tone. "I don't get it at all. Are you just politely telling me to push off?"

"No, no, not at all" said Vesta. "Ariadne, you tell this story very well. Please help Amy Elizabeth understand what we are talking about".

Ariadne nodded, smiled her sweetest goddess smile, and looked directly at Amy Elizabeth. She breathed in deeply, relaxed her body, and started her tale.

"The story starts thousands, and thousands of years ago. There weren't so many creatures living on the planet, and the gods thought it would be a good idea if they put one of the creatures in charge. So, they spent a long time talking to each one of the creatures. Then they made a list of all the abilities of each of the creatures, and they compared them.

The gods particularly wanted to find a creature that was calm, strong, loving, thoughtful and wise. It was the cat that came closest to everything they were looking for. They thought the cat would be perfect for controlling a wise, thoughtful planet, which is exactly what the gods were looking for. So, they had a big party with the cats, then gave them the power of speech, so they could communicate.

Things started well, but then problems started. Cats liked to enjoy life, and stretch out in the sun, and snooze. So sometimes a god would ask a cat what was going on. The cat would purr and reply lazily: "Brrrrr...I will find out tomorrow...or maybe the next day."

The gods got fed up with this. So, they decided to change the creature that was in charge. They had noticed that mankind was always busy, rushing around planning new things to do. They put mankind in charge.

The gods thought the cats would be disappointed. In fact, they were really pleased. More time to snooze! The gods thought mankind would be pleased. They were in charge and given the power of speech They were delighted and immediately started shouting and singing and running around.

Now not all the gods were convinced that mankind being in charge was a good idea. Some, like my ancestors, had doubts. They thought that mankind was so busy, sometimes they might get into trouble. So, my ancestors persuaded the other gods to allow cats to keep their Purr so they could tell the gods whether things were going well or very badly. And the gods were very clear to mankind.

"Don't forget," the gods warned, "If you mess things up, the cats will be back in control!"

"Will never happen!" all mankind chanted.

"And that, dear Amy Elizabeth" said Ariadne, "is the story behind cats."

"So, let me get this straight "said Amy Elizabeth "are you SuperHeroes seriously thinking of putting cats back in control?"

Vesta, in her business-like fashion, took the lead in answering:

"I know I speak for all the Surrey Hills SuperHeroes when I say we simply want to send mankind a message. We, the SuperHeroes, want to keep helping each other and you with all the efforts to keep the planet beautiful. But to keep our energy high, we need to let mankind know that everyone needs to help too. So, the warning will be out there: "Behave well and keep calm, or the cats will take over!"

For now, we will just arrange for certain cats to be around, and to be seen, and give a calming message when mankind looks like creating mischief. Make them think twice."

"Will these be normal house cats?" asked Amy Elizabeth, thinking of the small tabby that lounged about her home.

"Not at all" replied Vesta. "I have in mind very large cat like creatures. Beautiful, and black with glistening fur. And an ability to purr very loudly, almost like a big engine. Mankind won't know whether they are looking a house cat or a Puma Cat!"

"And I propose" said the Green Man, at last with enthusiasm in his voice "that we start this experiment in the place we all love most. The Surrey Hills. That way all Surrey Hills SuperHeroes can plainly see how much this Puma Cat plan brings to our beautiful area."

FOUR YEARS LATER. KYLE AND DAKSHA. GUILDFORD.

The memory of that crazy, scary night in the Guildford Castle Gardens, has become a distant one now for Kyle and Daksha. However, they both recognize its importance. After the experience they have become bit by bit a little more serious. More focused but without losing their sense of fun. They both care more now. For the environment in which they live, for the planet and for each other.

Kyle has his own landscape gardening business. He specializes in gardens that promote a healthy environment. He has lots of customers and is booked out for months to come.

Daksha makes money by working on open–air markets. She works for one company that makes environmentally friendly skin creams and another which makes drinks that are good for your health. Her favourite, however, is selling fresh fruit and vegetables. She particularly likes shouting out the special offers, when it comes to clearing unsold produce at the end of the day. She is really good at that!

Kyle and Daksha share a small house in the centre of town. They can both get tired and stressed after a hard week at work. When things get a little too hectic, they spend time with their small black cat. They call her Serena. When they look into her deep, sapphire eyes, the planet seems a calmer, better, more beautiful place.

Places mentioned in this story: -

Guildford Town Centre.
You can find many great restaurants, coffee shops and pubs along the famous cobbled High Street and surrounding alleys and smaller roads. Great shopping too, including stores specialising in environmentally friendly products.

Market Days are Fridays and Saturdays on North Street. Watch out for Daksha shouting out her special offers in the late afternoon!

There are also several specialist markets on the High Street, including an outstanding monthly Farmers Market. Look out for Gemma and her wonderful skin creams.

Pitch Hill.
This is a sandstone spur that rises from Peaslake. Great walking, with fabulous views to the South Downs. George Harrison's Here comes the Sun song was inspired by the views.

Guildford Castle and Grounds.
Guildford Castle and gardens are close to Guildford Centre, opposite the top of Tunsgate. The Castle was built by the Normans, just after the 1066 invasion. The Castle, and stunning Castle gardens can be visited. Check for timings, and do not try to visit after hours!

The statue of Alice through the Looking Glass is in a walled garden, inside the castle grounds, near the house that Lewis Carroll used to rent.

The story which Ariadne tells about the gods putting first cats and then mankind in charge, is based upon a very old Chinese fable. There are many versions of this. I have heard many variations on my travels. You can find one on www.cuteness.com/blog/content/cat-folklore-legends-from-around-the-world

Reports of sightings of the Surrey Panther are many and various. They date from 1830, and reports continue today.

THE SURREY SUPERHEROES AND THE STAR FROM AFAR

CHAPTER 1. THERE'S SOMETHING IN THE AIR.

Strangely perhaps, it was Wally the Walrus who first noticed that things were changing.

Wally was back in the Arctic, back on his beloved ice shelf. His long and exciting journeys seemed far in the past though he still enjoyed the memories: the fishermen he had met in Ireland, his visit to France, his mega-scary swim to the Scilly Isles, his dramatic adventures there, and his long journey home. All these things he thought about every day. Well, perhaps to be more accurate, he thought about them once he had eaten a big breakfast of clams and seafood. And he thought about them for at least a couple of minutes before he dropped off for a nice twelve-hour sleep.

There was one thing, one person, he thought about a lot. Not as much as he thought about eating seafood, but still a lot. Eleanor, the lady who had saved him from the fury of the red-faced man in the Scillies. Eleanor, the lady who was known as Eleanor the Invisible. Eleanor who had a complete understanding of water and who had travelled the world, using her magical powers for the good of all people. Eleanor who had made Wally an Honorary Surrey Hills SuperHero. Eleanor who had given Wally the secret code

word SHISH for if he needed to contact other SuperHeroes. Eleanor and her amazing abilities had made a big impression on Wally.

This particular morning, Wally had enjoyed a particularly large seafood meal. And as his munching stopped, he began to think that he should get in touch with Eleanor using the SHISH contact code. There was something on his mind. Something he thought might be very important. Something he thought Eleanor and the other SuperHeroes might know more about.

That something was temperature. You see, Wally lived in the Arctic so he was used to the cold. Wally slept on a bed of ice so he had to be used to low temperatures. For a long, long time, before his great adventure, Wally had noticed that temperatures in the Arctic were going up. Little by little, year by year, it was getting warmer. In fact, it was the increase in temperature that started Wally's big adventure. The ice on which Wally had lived broke off the Arctic and drifted out into the open ocean. It had broken off because some of the ice had melted and Wally's old home became a small ice island.

But now, since Wally's return, things had changed. Things weren't getting warmer any more. That was for sure. And little by little, over the months, Wally became convinced it was getting colder. Not that Wally was complaining. As the temperature fell, it seemed like there were even more shellfish to feed on and Wally liked that. In addition, Wally felt he slept better and longer when it was cold. Wally certainly appreciated that. It was just that Wally had learned how important temperature was during his big voyage. Eleanor and Wally had talked a lot about it on the Scilly isles.

So, Wally thought it would be good to get in touch with Eleanor, let her know his thoughts, and tell her what he was experiencing. He thought it was the responsible thing to do. He felt it was his duty to repay all the help Eleanor had given him on his travels. So Wally prepared to activate the SHISH code and to contact his old friend.

Just as Wally was preparing to make contact, Eleanor was in her favourite place, the beautiful Surrey Hills. It was Eleanor's favourite time of year. Early May. Normally, this was the time when swimming in the ponds and rivers was at its best. Water fresh and invigorating. No longer the blasts of biting cold wind to endure after winter bathing. That was a normal May, but this year was not normal. This year, Eleanor couldn't even get into some of the ponds. There was thick ice over the surface. Brave as ever, Eleanor did make a hole in the ice and dipped in. The dip only lasted a few seconds! Things were changing in the Hills.

Thousands of miles to the south in Cape Town, South Africa, the southern summer was fading into autumn. Vesta, Goddess of Fire was visiting, working with local Rangers, putting plans in place to avoid the horrendous fires which often raged in the area. Vesta's great gifts were the ability to create fire with one hand – KAPOW! and to freeze fire with the other- KAPOW! KAPOW! She used these gifts to help demonstrate to others how fire can be controlled. Recently, Vesta had found it much easier to freeze fire. When it came to creating fire, however, she found it more and more difficult. It seemed to require so much energy. At first, Vesta put this down to her great old age. Then she began to think it might have more to do with the temperature which seemed to be getting colder. As she thought about this, she looked up at Table Mountain. On the top, there was a thin layer of snow in the month of May.

That same day, Ariadne woke slowly from a deep sleep in a most comfortable bed. She had been helping a poor woman who had badly injured herself in a fall on a country path. As she regained consciousness, Ariadne heard the wind howling outside and felt its chill on her face through the open window. Ariadne was convinced she was still in the brisk climate of the Highlands of Scotland, where the injured woman lived. Then she remembered that, overnight, she had journeyed back to Crete in the normally balmy Mediterranean.

Back in the woods and hills of Surrey, the Green Man felt there was a lot going on. It confused him. The good news was that litter in the Surrey Hills was reducing. His work with Amy Elizabeth was paying off. The confusing news was that it was May and there was no sight of new leaves budding or of bluebells blooming. After thousands of years guarding the forests, this was all a bit much for the Green Man.

Grace the Dragon was finding that she could now only breathe fire with great difficulty. She had to spend about ten minutes in warm-up exercises first. Her ability to impress wrongdoers was significantly reduced.

The two young dinosaurs, Montmorency the Second and Montmorency the Third, were completely changed characters. Before, their unending energy had tormented and exhausted their poor parents. Their energetic rock throwing had created many of the outstanding features of the Surrey Hills. Recently, they had become tired and lazy They complained that it was too cold to wrestle or wade in the river They found throwing snowballs was much less exciting than throwing rocks. Some days their parents couldn't get them out of bed at all. They said they needed to stay where they were to keep warm.

Daksha who had partied with Kyle in Guildford Castle Grounds one crazy night had worked right through the Christmas and New Year outdoor markets. In some ways, they were the most exciting markets ever. They were all on frozen ponds or rivers. The markets on the frozen Wey and Thames were particularly exciting.

The Puma Cats, brought in by the SuperHeroes to help keep calm in the Surrey Hills, practically refused to go out any more. They stayed in the warm and slept and slept, and then slept and slept again.

Zac who had helped Farmer Fred Goodfellow with his computer issues had delved further into technology. He started to use his skills to help him understand the universe better. It became a big hobby. He got an app to help him stargaze. He became familiar with far away galaxies, the constellations in the Milky Way, the solar system, asteroid clouds and meteors. Then recently, he noticed something new. Something unexplained, apparently moving towards Planet Earth.

CHAPTER 2. A LITTLE LIGHT AND A LOT OF DARKNESS.

Eleanor was not surprised by what Wally had to say when he called from the Arctic. All the gossip among the SuperHeroes suggested that something was going on. Something important. Something that impacted the environment of the entire planet. The truth was, however, that none of the SuperHeroes had the full picture and no one had a clear plan for dealing with whatever was going on.

At the end of their chat, Eleanor and Wally agreed that they needed to get all the SuperHeroes together on a Shishoom conference. (That's a special conferencing system set up by Zac for the SuperHeroes.) The date was set for the northern Summer Solstice, June 21, an ideal time to get light on to the problem. Meantime, all SuperHeroes were asked to observe things carefully, note what was going on and prepare presentations for the upcoming Shishoom event.

By SuperHero standards, the conference was a remarkably serious, business-like affair. Everyone had well prepared, clear presentations. There was almost no gossiping or joking; even the young dinosaurs were well behaved and calm.

In summary, the message was simple. Everywhere there were clear signs that the planet's temperature was no longer rising. It was getting colder. There were signs that things were accelerating. It was getting colder faster and that was having a big impact on the environment. None of the SuperHeroes knew why this was happening.

Zac's input, using his stargazing app, was particularly concerning. There was definitely a new, large object in the sky. It was moving towards Planet Earth. The strange thing was, Zac couldn't tell exactly what sort of an object it was. It didn't seem to be another planet, or a meteor or even a satellite.

There was much discussion and debate. One really important conclusion was reached. The temperatures and the object in the sky were connected in some way. Nobody in the SuperHero group had the skills to understand why there was a connection. So until everything was fully understood, no sensible program of action could be put in place.

The SuperHeroes agreed they needed specialist input from some scientists. Zac and Ariadne were asked to seek out help from experts at the Scientific Study Centre in the Surrey Hills and to get back to the group with all speed. The situation was alarming and urgent. No time to be lost.

CHAPTER 3. A LOT OF SCIENCE AND A LOT OF RED TAPE.

Zac immersed himself in researching the right people to meet at the campus of the Scientific Study Centre in the Surrey Hills. He knew he needed an expert in climate and another in astrophysics. He searched long and hard, read biographies and reviews and finally came up with two names that he felt had the necessary expertise.

Professor Wetherby-Good seemed to Zac to have all the right qualifications. She had studied Climatology in universities in Australia and Canada, so had done studies into the effects of extreme heat and cold. She had undertaken practical projects in China and Saharan Africa and had seen changing weather patterns at first hand. She was now head of department at the Scientific Study Centre.

Dr Akito Ake was a rising star in astrophysics. He had studied at a University in Tokyo, and then moved on to manage practical space exploration projects in the United States. He was widely published and was a much sought-after speaker. He was on a year-long special assignment in the Surrey Hills.

If Zac thought finding the right people was laborious, trying to get an appointment for a meeting was something else. Zac wrote directly and was very clear about his objectives and what he wanted to talk about. Messages and e-mails were passed on to secretaries and assistants. There was much "Hum"-ing and "Ha"-ing and a lot of "I'm afraid he's very busy" or "She's in a very important meeting right now." The scientific experts didn't seem to find Zac's messages very important. He felt there was almost a reluctance to meet.

Finally, Zac took the bull by the horns and found out where each of the experts lived. He went to their houses, knocked on the door, politely explained the situation and refused to leave until a meeting date was set. It worked. A date and time were fixed.

Ariadne and Zac presented themselves at the designated Scientific Study building on the agreed date and time. They had been told to bring personal identification with them. Easier for Zac who had a passport than for Ariadne since goddesses didn't need passports. Instead, Ariadne brought a letter of recommendation from the lady she had been helping in Scotland.

They were met at the entrance by a large, rather dour looking man, in a very dour grey suit. He insisted on checking their backpacks. Then in silence, he escorted them to the basement of the building. There, in a small meeting room, they met Wetherby-Good, and Akito for the first time.

Wetherby-Good was tall and blonde, casually dressed in a designer athletic suit. Akito was slim and powerfully built. He wore a smart suit, white shirt and stylish tie. His black hair was groomed in the latest style – very sharp!

Both experts had open, kind faces. Yet the atmosphere in the room was cold, formal, restrained.

"Look, in all honesty, we can't talk to you unless you sign the OSA." Akito opened the conversation sharply.

"OSA?" said Zac. "OSA!" What in the name of gorgeous gardens is the OSA?"

"The OSA is the Official Secrets Act," said Akito, still very business-like.

"The Official Secrets Act!" said Zac, "who do you think I am, James Bond?"

"Actually," chimed in Wetherby-Good in a warmer tone, "actually, I think you'd make rather a good James Bond."

Akito got the conversation back to a business-like tone. "We can only talk to you if you agree that nothing that is said goes out of this room. If you don't sign the document, the meeting ends here and now. That's the way that the PTBs want it, so that's that."

"PTBs!" Zac, normally so calm, was getting rattled. "Where do PTBs come from and whatever do they do?"

"PTBs are the Powers That Be. Our bosses. Like I said, if you don't sign the document, it's meeting over."

"I don't get it" said Zac, "we come here all friendly and concerned and you guys treat us like we're spies or something…."

Wetherby-Good cut through Zac's rant in a calm voice. She looked particularly towards Ariadne as she spoke: "I would like to offer a word of welcome to you both today. I know we are not easy people to reach and tie down. We'll touch on that later.

For the moment, there are some things we need to deal with. Akito and I both know that the things you have been observing are things that we need to discuss. We also know an action plan is desperately needed. We know about the Surrey Hills SuperHeroes, we have researched you and you have some extraordinary talent. Akito and I have great knowledge and technological power at our disposal. We need to talk with you and you need to talk with us and the whole planet needs us to talk together.

However, I can totally assure you that if you don't sign the famous Official Secrets Act, agreeing not to tell others of our chat, nothing will happen. There are people in this building who will check we have the signed document the moment you leave. If we don't, we will be dismissed immediately, and you will be deprived of all our resources. So, the choice is simple. Sign or say goodbye!"

"Thank you for your welcome," replied Ariadne. "We have one important point to make. If our conversation leads to action which I'm sure it will, we will have to involve the other SuperHeroes. So how does that figure with the famous OSA?"

Wetherby–Good smiled sweetly and winked her left eye. "Ariadne, I will deny ever saying these words but listen carefully. Technically, if the OSA is broken, the Powers That Be will pursue the law breakers through the Law Courts. But I really doubt that even our bureaucratic, pompous Powers will try and prosecute a Green Man who has been around from the start of time or a goddess who can make and freeze fire or a couple of crazy dinosaurs or a dragon or cats who look like pumas and who calm things down. No, I think you are pretty safe."

Ariadne and Zac looked at each other, nodded and smiled, and signed the document that was on the table.

"Excellent" said Akito, "I suggest we begin. Our story is fairly simple.

The observations of the SuperHeroes are correct. There is a large object travelling towards Planet Earth. The presence of the object is severely changing the weather. The object is having the effect of shielding Earth from the Sun's warmth so temperatures are getting lower. If and when the object passes by the Earth, things will go back to normal. If you can call Global Warming normal.

And that, believe it or not, is all we are sure of. The reason? When we first noticed the changes, we alerted the Powers. They were immediately petrified by the chaos and unhappiness that would arise if the news of the object in space and the impact it was having became public knowledge. So we were banned from doing any more research and we were prohibited from talking to the newspapers about what was happening.

The "official line" for anyone who notices the object in the sky or who realizes that it is getting colder is this. "There is an object in the sky, but don't worry, everything is under control. The object is a tiny fragment of a far-off star that burned out years ago. It will not collide with Planet Earth, it will simply pass by at a distance. In the meantime, it will feel a little cooler, so just wear an extra sweater until things warm up again. Don't worry, the PTBS have got the Star from Afar completely under control."

That's about all we know" said Akito. "Not a lot, is it! So, I'll leave it to Professor Wetherby- Good to tell you everything we don't know."

"Get your pencils and notepads out" said the Professor. "I have a long list.

We don't know what the object in space is. We don't know where it comes from. We don't know what the object is made of. Whether it's metal or plastic or rock or gaseous or a mixture. We haven't a clue.

We don't know how big the object is. We are not really sure of the shape although we suspect from our early work that there may be two objects together. One smaller, one larger.

We don't know" and here her tone became a little more sinister "we don't know if the object is simply flying through space or whether it is being controlled by intelligent beings.

Because we don't know any of these things, we cannot know if the so-called Star from Afar will collide with Planet Earth or not. And we cannot calculate when the object will hit Earth or pass by.

It is clear we need to find all these things out. We need to, urgently, to ensure the survival of the planet. We have the knowledge and equipment to analyse the Star from Afar and get to the truth. However, we have been banned from doing so. If we gave the slightest impression of using our technology to find out more, we would be fired, perhaps imprisoned. So, this is why we need the help of the SuperHeroes."

Both Ariadne and Zac were taken aback by this last statement.

"Look" said Zac. "The SuperHeroes are all up for sustaining the beauty of our planet, especially in the Surrey Hills. But as you know, we are a very assorted bunch. From goddesses to dragons, dinosaurs, even a walrus. None of us has the know-how, or the scientific equipment to really help."

"Here's what we propose", said Akito. "We will give you the tools and help you finish the job.

We will give you the ability to probe into space. To see the Star from Afar clearly. We have a telescope at this Science Centre we can loan you. It's not a modern radio telescope like we currently use in our work. It's fifty years old and uses reflecting optical lenses. Right now, it's simply standing behind this building where it was placed, out of sight, when we got the latest digital space telescope. It's dirty and rusty; it needs cleaning up. And it's very heavy. You need to get it to a high place in the Hills, give it some care and you will be amazed what a powerful instrument it is.

Once you have the telescope working, you need to relay all the information to us, so we can process it and understand it on our powerful computer."

"That is the tricky bit" Professor Wetherby added to the conversation. "If we are seen to be receiving information from outside or using our computer to analyse the data, it will be game over. For us, for you, and probably for the whole planet. So, Zac" she said, looking straight at him "you will have to transfer the data via your Shishoom technology. It will be hard work, but we think you can do it. Via Shishoom, only we will be able to see the information.

Once we start receiving the information, Akito and I will go into the party business. Parties are greatly encouraged by the PTBs as a way to keep everyone happy. Lots to eat and drink, lots of dancing and singing.

Every time we want to use our computing power on the information you provide, we will announce another party at the Science Centre. Believe me, people will be far too concerned about having a good time to worry about what we are up to."

Zac and Ariadne were hugely impressed by the cleverness of the planning. The future became at the same time both exciting and very stressful.

"We are with you." said Zac. "You can count on us one hundred per cent. We'll get all the other Surrey Hills SuperHeroes on side as fast as we can!"

"There is no time to lose" said Akito. "The first job is to get that telescope to a high place in the Hills so you can start your work. The thing is, you will have to move it without a whole load of noise and fuss and you will have to move it at night, so nobody sees. But I'm sure that will be no problem for the SuperHeroes!"

CHAPTER 4. HEAVY RUMOURS AND AN EVEN HEAVIER TELESCOPE.

Akito suggested that they take a look at the old telescope straight away so that they could plan how to move it. Akito checked the coast was clear, took them through the basement and then opened a door that led to a patch of land at the back of he building.

In front of them, a large object covered by an old, grey, rotting tarpaulin. Zac guessed the object must be nearly three metres high and about two metres in width. Akito pulled off the tarpaulin. There was the telescope, mounted on a circular base. There was a system of cogs driven by a wheel that was designed to adjust the angle of the scope. The whole structure was made of metal. As far as Zac could see through the dirt and rust, the base was in iron, the scope itself in copper. It was imposing, a relic from another age.

Zac whistled through his teeth. "That's got to be very, very heavy!" He said. "That's not going to be easy to move."

"You're right" said Akito. "Unfortunately, we've lost all the records so I've no way of checking what the actual weight is. But I can tell you that once you have it cleaned up, this is a beautiful piece of kit. We can only emphasize, speed is vital. So, make your plans as soon as you can."

Ariadne and Zac were full of excitement and energy as they prepared to say their goodbyes. Zac was already thinking about ways of moving the heavy telescope. Yet there was one question that still troubled him. He had hesitated to ask as he felt it might destroy the team spirit they had started to build. Then he decided to get everything clear and open.

"Look friends," he said "before we leave, I do have one question to ask you. I know you said that all the stuff about the Star from Afar and the colder temperatures is very hush-hush. But do you think that rumours may have leaked out? Are we the only group to have suspected something?"

"We are glad you asked that question." replied Professor Wetherby-Good. "We hadn't mentioned this before because we didn't want to scare you. But we can see you are tough SuperHeroes, and you need to know everything. There are rumours of a group of powerful, determined individuals who seek every opportunity to make money. They don't care how they make money, good things or bad, and they seem to prefer bad things. They are ruthless. There are rumours that they have spies and informers everywhere. Perhaps in this Science Centre, perhaps even among the Powers That Be.

These are just rumours, nothing proven. So just be careful and keep your eyes and ears open."

Zac and Ariadne parted at the Science Centre and they agreed that Zac should plan the next steps. He walked home, his mind buzzing.

"Hello there!" he greeted Aisha on arrival, then he was straight on the Shishoom.

The Green Man, Farmer Fred Goodfellow, Montmorency the second, Montmorency the third and Kyle all agreed to meet him at the Science Centre the next evening at 7pm sharp. The meeting place was the small piece of ground on which the old telescope stood. Zac also put in a call to several of the Puma Cats. Finally, Zac told the whole SuperHero team about his plan.

Zac was so busy the next day, thinking and planning, that he could hardly concentrate on work. Finally, leaving time arrived and Zac set off for the Science Centre. Good to their word, everyone was there on time.

Fred Goodfellow arrived as promised on a farm cart drawn by two magnificent Fjord horses borrowed from a local farm. The Green Man brought a large pulley system, the frame made of the strongest timber. He had constructed it that afternoon and used ropes from Kyle's landscaping business. Zac opened the meeting.

"Okay, SuperHeroes. Welcome and here's the plan. As you know, we have to get this telescope to Leith Hill, the highest point for miles around. We have to move it with the minimum of fuss or noise and ensure we don't draw attention to ourselves. The route I have chosen is via the Greensand Way, which we will pick up just south of Shamley Green. From there, we can travel to Leith Hill without anyone seeing us. We need to reach the top of the Hill by 7am tomorrow morning so we can hide the telescope before there are people around.

First, we need to load the cart with the telescope. This is going to be very tough work. So the Green Man will set up his pulley system and Kyle will fix the ropes around the telescope. The two Montmorencies, the Green Man and Kyle will be at the other end

of the pulley ropes and do the heaving. I will steady the telescope and make sure it's placed straight on the cart. Fred Goodfellow will hold the horses steady.

In five minutes, all was ready. Everyone - horses, cart and pulley - were in the right place.

"Ready, team." Zac cried "One, two, three, HEEEEEAVE!"

The pulling team gave it their all. The Montmorencies and the Green Man had SuperHero strength. The ropes and the pulley frame creaked with the strain put on them.

But nothing! The telescope stayed where it had been for the last fifty years.

"Okay, guys. Rest!" cried Zac. "I'll join the rope team. We'll give it one more go.

One, two, three, SUPERHEROHEEAVE!!!!"

Nothing. They gave it four more goes but still nothing. It seemed like the great plan to save Planet Earth had fallen at the first hurdle. Heads began to drop.

Then Farmer Fred Goodfellow called over to Zac, his voice calm and authorative through many years of working with heavy loads on the farm.

"Why don't we do this, Zac?" he suggested. "We'll unhook the Fjord Horses and put them on the pulling team. I'll put the brake on the cart and make sure it doesn't budge. I reckon that will do the job!"

Five more minutes of rearranging and they were ready.

"One, two, three. SUPER MEGA SUPERHEROHEEEEEAVE!"

The old telescope finally lifted from the ground. There was a tearing sound as the plants and roots that had grown around the base were ripped away. Then slowly, gradually, SuperHero muscles straining to the limit, the telescope was lifted on to cart in perfect position.

The team collapsed on the ground as soon as the weight was gone. That is, all of the team except the Fjord Horses who still looked totally calm and relaxed.

"Lush!" said Kyle. "I knew we could do it."

"Well done, team" cried Zac. "But we've already lost time. So, Fred, please hook the horses back on the cart. Kyle, can you and the Green Man please secure the telescope with ropes.

Dinosaurs and Green Man, please make your way to the Greensand Way at Shamley Green by a countryside route.

The cart will have to pass through Guildford to reach the Greensand Way. We'll have to travel by regular roads. There's no alternative that will work for the cart and its big load. Fred, Kyle and I will put the tarpaulin over the Scope and stay with it on the journey to Shamley.

I'm hoping the Fjord Horses will catch all the attention as we go around Guildford. If we get questions, we'll say we're on a training run for an important Horse Show.

Good luck everyone. See you at the Shamley Green staging point!"

Zac was right about the journey around Guildford. It was the Fjord Horses that attracted most of the attention. Lots of admiration for the beautiful beasts as they passed restaurants and pubs and practically zero interest in what was under the tarpaulin on the cart. So the Shamley Green staging point was reached in reasonable time and there they hooked up again with the Dinosaurs and the Green Man.

Zac jumped off the cart just before they got onto the Greensand Way to have a brief conference with the Green Man who of course knew the countryside well. The light was beginning to fade as they started to chat.

"Look." said the Green Man "We should be able to get though to Leith Hill okay. But there will be places where the path will be narrow and the height of the telescope will come up against low hanging branches. So I suggest I go ahead and clear the way where needed. The rest stay with the cart. Have the Montmorencies walk behind in case a big shove is needed from time to time."

Just as he finished, there was a rustling in the bushes near the path. A large black shape with gleaming eyes emerged. The group froze. The Fjord Horses immediately became uneasy.

Only Zac was unaffected by this sudden appearance. He walked over, and grinned at a large Surrey Puma Cat.

"It's good to see you again." he said. "We appreciate you being here tonight keeping a watch out. What news do you have?"

"The rrrroute to Leith Hill is prrrretty clear." purred this Puma Cat. "I have fourrrr other cats posted along the way, keeping a look out forrrr you. All is calm at the moment. But there arrrre those who watch you. Be carrrreful."

The Puma Cat disappeared back into the bushes as quickly as it had appeared. A sense of calm was left behind and the group gained confidence as they set out on the Greensand Way.

The journey that night was tough though largely uneventful. Everyone knew they had to press on to meet the deadline that had been set for getting the telescope in place on the top of the Hill. They stopped only to give the Green Man time to clear overhanging branches, and occasionally to take drinks of tea from the flasks that Zac had brought along. The route took them over Winterfold Heath once owned by a great Tudor King. Then passed Holmbury

Hill, and through Leith Hill Wood. They saw no one along the way. Occasionally Both Zac and Kyle noticed slight movement in the dark forest. Perhaps the glint of eyes watching them. They both convinced themselves it was simply the Puma Cats keeping watch.

Finally, weary from the long travel and the lack of sleep, they arrived at the foot of Leith Hill. They had about an hour and a half to get up the hill, get the telescope off the cart and hide it from view. The ascent started well. Then disaster struck. It had been a cold night and, as they got higher on the Hill, there was snow on the paths. It became very slippery. Nobody, not even the Fjord Horses, could get a grip underfoot. Everyone, including Dinosaurs, Green Man, Kyle and Zac, was pushing and shoving and slipping. The cart just wasn't making progress anymore. It even started slipping backwards. Fred Goodfellow became concerned that the weight of the telescope in these treacherous conditions might even tip the cart over. Time was ticking away but they had to stop.

Farmer Goodfellow placed rocks behind the cart wheels to stop the cart slipping backwards. Zac tried to find a way forward. He was sure he had used all the muscle power at his disposal to push and pull the cart up the slippery hill and he had failed. Soon they would be seen and the whole plan would fail. Despondency began to mount. Heads dropped.

Kyle walked over to Zac and talked quietly to him. "Have you really used all the muscle power available to the SuperHeroes?"

Zac realised what Kyle was talking about. In an instant, he was on Shishoom on his iPhone. His conversation with Grace was short and effective.

In exactly twelve minutes and thirty-two seconds, Grace the Dragon landed on Leith Hill, just a few metres in front of the immobile cart. Kyle had his longest rope ready, one end already tied very firmly around the front axle of the cart. Kyle then ran the rope around and over Grace's left shoulder. Grace opened her enormous jaws, and Kyle inserted the end of the rope from the right-hand side. Grace clamped down hard. There was no way that rope was going to move!

Fred Goodfellow made sure the Fjord Horses were ready. Zac and Kyle got everyone else (including the Montmorencies who had started a snowball fight) ready to shove behind the wagon.

Then, "ONE, TWO, THREE. MEGASUPERHERODRAGONPOWER!!!"

Grace powered into the air, her great wings creating huge air currents which cleared the snow off the whole area. The rope tensed, the cart eased forward. The Fjord Horses, unfazed by the presence of a huge dragon, surged forward with new energy. The Dinosaurs, who regarded Grace as somewhere between a football superstar and a Hollywood legend, pushed and shoved and scrummed behind the cart as never before.

Cart and telescope went up the Hill at warp speed. In honesty, Zac and Kyle struggled to keep up and the roller coaster ride of the cart made Farmer Goodfellow feel physically ill! Meanwhile, a few of the Puma Cats looking on, wondering what all the hub-bub was about.

Cart and telescope reached the top. The Superheroes had just twenty minutes left to get the telescope off the cart, place it behind Leith Tower, and hide it with branches.

Zac took charge and got everyone organised. Grace was released as soon as possible. (She did tend to draw attention.)

"Talk to you later, Grace." shouted Zac. "Couldn't have done it without Dragon Power!"

"See you soon." Grace called back, as her huge wings powered her into the air.

They used the same procedure to winch the telescope off the cart as they had to lift it on. This time, with gravity on their side, life was much easier. Farmer Goodfellow then immediately set off with the cart for home. The Montmorencies, finally tired out, accompanied him.

Zac and Kyle and the Green Man raced around the area for all the fallen branches they could find. Within fifteen minutes, they had covered the telescope tarpaulin with natural vegetation.

The Green Man left quickly, again to avoid attention. Then just as Kyle and Zac threw the last branches on, two hikers reached the summit of Leith Hill.

"Morning lads." called one of the hikers. "Nice quiet, calm morning!"

"Yes, indeed. Plenty of scope for quiet here!" replied Kyle.

Kyle and Zac had a big day before them. They had been up all night and they suddenly realised what was before them. They both had to get home, show their faces at work, then get back that evening to work on restoring the telescope. There was no choice. It was that or the plan to save the planet failed.

Meanwhile Grace, always a sensitive dragon, began to think about the tasks facing the SuperHeroes as soon as she was airborne. She was concerned about Zac and Kyle in particular. They had to get the telescope working quickly. They both had jobs in the daytime and they still needed to get home. So, when she spied a really quiet place on the path down the hill, she swooped and landed, waited for Kyle and Zac, then offered them rides home.

"Lush" said Kyle. "But take it easy on the flight."

"Sorry." said Grace. "Taking it easy is not what I do."

CHAPTER 5. WAKE UP AND SMELL THE COFFEE.

It was coffee that kept Zac and Kyle going over the next days. Coffee, and the excitement of doing something that could save the planet. They continued with their day jobs. No option. Rent to pay and food to buy. After work, they would rush home and get a precious two- or three-hours sleep.

Then they both prepared packed suppers and lots of strong coffee in thermos flasks.

Grace continued to play an essential role. She would pick them both up on Shalford Park in the early evening, then fly them over to Leith Hill. Nice and gently, at the special request of Kyle.

Work on the telescope went well. The first evening back, they took cleaning products for metal and vinegar for glass lenses plus a pile of cleaning cloths and a big can of lubricating oil.

That night's work was physically tough. Once they had checked with the Puma Cats who continued to keep watch, they paused only for coffee and to eat their suppers. The dirt and rust on the telescope took a lot of shifting and masses of "elbow grease." But by the time Grace arrived at sunrise, the telescope was clean and the adjustment mechanism was working. They were ready to observe the heavens, most particularly the Star from Afar, as soon as darkness fell again. They covered and camouflaged the telescope, climbed on Grace's broad back, hung on to her neck and flew home for a day's work!

Spirits were high as they landed on the top of the hill for a second night of work on the telescope. At last, they could get a close look at the "Star". Zac could add even more to the flow of information he was already passing via Shishoom and the Stargazing WhatsApp to Dr Wetherby-Good and Akito at the Science Centre. On top of that, Grace had brought take-away pizza for them to share. One more night after this and they would be at the weekend and some well-earned rest! Perhaps they were close to a big breakthrough on their save the planet project.

Their spirits fell when they went around the back of Leith Tower to uncover the telescope. Many of the branches had been pulled away and half a dozen placards were stuck on the tarpaulin. The placards had ugly handwritten messages scrawled on them.

"WHAT THE BLAZES IS THIS DOING HERE?" read one.

"SAY NO TO TELESCOPE SPIES IN SURREY" another.

"SAVE OUR STAR FROM AFAR."

"BRASSERS RULE- OK"

Zac and Kyle looked at each other. There was something aggressive, intimidating in what they saw. They went to find the Puma Cat who had been on duty that night.

"I saw what happened" said the Puma Cat who they found sitting calmly admiring the sunset. "You should be concerned, but not too concerrrned.

I saw the placards being put on the telescope by kids. About ten or twelve rrrrrowdy teenagers. They came in the late afternoon. They might have done more, even damaged the telescope, if I hadn't gone over and had a quiet word with them. They were prretty scarred when they saw me and calmed down immediately. They told me they had met a man in a coffee bar who had paid them lots of cash to make this protest. He had given them the placards and told them where to find the telescope. They won't be back. I can guarantee that. But others might. You should finish your work quickly."

Zac and Kyle were re-assured that one of the Puma Cats would stay on watch all night and they were determined to finish their work.

They got the telescope working immediately and, for the first time saw in close up, the detail of the famous Star from Afar. What a revelation! What amazing news to report to Akito and Dr Wetherby- Good!

– ■ –

Earlier that same day, Daksha was taking a well-earned a coffee break in Farnham Town Centre. She was in town for a market and had done well during the morning selling her locally grown fresh vegetables and fruit. As temperatures dropped, fruit was becoming more and more difficult to find. But Daksha had manged to secure some tasty Surrey apples and they sold quickly.

By nature, Daksha was sunny and positive. That's what made her so effective on the market places. Today though, her mood was restrained. Kyle had become closely involved with the SuperHero team, working on understanding the famous Star from Afar. In fact, she had hardly seen him recently, as he helped Zac set up some telescope in the Surrey Hills. All very hush-hush, and very demanding. Kyle hadn't even come back from his night's work on the telescope, when she got up at five this morning to be ready for the market.   Still, the weekend was not far off, and Kyle had assured her things would calm down a bit.

She was in an intriguing café. The coffee was good and the design of the interior was a replica of a traditional library. Shelves covered the walls right up to the high ceiling; books and magazines filled the shelves. If you wanted, you could purchase some of the books or magazines.

The café attracted an interesting crowd. A party of four sitting to her right particularly caught her attention. She avoided staring, but the group was striking. Two men. One older. Large head with pronounced features and very short grey hair. Expensively dressed in a designer suit and a huge bling-bling luxury designer watch on his wrist. Next to him, an enormously tall younger man with an athletic build. A huge, colourful bandana tied around his dreadlocks. From his accent, Daksha guessed of Caribbean origin. From his appearance maybe a basketball star?

Sitting opposite them, two women. One, young, tanned and incredibly muscular. She had a jewelled patch over her right eye and the words "World Wrestling Champion" tattooed on the inside of her left wrist. The appearance of the other woman could accurately be described as "The return of Marilyn Monroe." Except this lady had a silver knuckleduster on her right hand.

From casually listening to their chat, Daksha got to know their names which suited them really well. Oligarch, the boss man with the huge bling- bling designer watch; Hoops, the tall guy with the bandana; Lady Wrestler, the muscular lady with a tattoo; and Marilyn with a Fist. All very obvious, all pretty frightening. None she would ever want to meet in a dark alley. Little did she know then how important these people would become in the lives of the SuperHeroes.

Daksha was about to leave the coffee shop, when Oligarch started a serious conversation with the others. He spoke quietly but clearly and with great conviction. Daksha immediately understood that he was the leader of the group. She stayed where she was, paying huge attention to the dregs at the bottom of her cup and listening with great care.

Oligarch's English was fluent, his accent a mixture of eastern European and East End London.

"We always have to remember" he started "what we are good at. And we have to stick with what we are good at. Because not only are we good at it, we are the best at it!

We know how to make money out of all the things that nobody else wants. All the stuff they don't want no more, all the rubbish, all the things they've bought and don't like, we find ways of making money from it.

We make lots of dosh! Lots of mullah! Lots of lovely money! We don't pretend to be nice people. We don't let other people get in our way. If there's rubbish around, we'll find a way of making money. So, the more rubbish, the more dosh. We love rubbish. Rubbish makes us rich!

People in the North of England used to say, "where there's muck, there's brass!" In other words, rubbish means money. That's how we got the name of our little gang "The Brassers."

So, I got you together here today, not only to generously buy you all coffee but to talk about this Star from Afar that people are blabbing on about.

I am blooming sure there's money to be made here. That there thing, up there in the sky, let it come! I say. Let it hit the Earth, if that's what it's going to do. If it does, there will be a whole load of rubbish and muck everywhere. And who will make lots of dosh out of the muck and rubbish? We will. The Brassers will!

I've got friends right at the top of the Powers That Be. Very close friends. Lots of them. Friends who listen to me. I've told them "don't mess with the Star from Afar. Let it come – we'll all make money when it does." And they agree with me. You can see their tongues are hanging out at the thought of more lovely dosh headed their way.

Now then." Oligarch paused to stare intently, one by one, at each of the others. "Now then. Not everyone is sensible, like us. There are wishy-washy, smarty-pants people out there who think they know better than us. Better than the Brassers!" He snorted. "We know there's a bunch of do-gooders that are trying to find out more about our Star from Afar. Then maybe try and stop it. Let me tell you, we already know all that we need to know about our Star. It will make us money! Bring it on!

So instead of them stopping the Star, we are going to stop them spoiling our fun. There's a group of them who have slyly and secretly, under the cover of dark, put an old telescope on top of Leith Hill. I am sure they are spying on our Star. Probably they'll soon tell us it's made of green cheese or some rubbish like that. I've already paid a bunch of yahoo layabout teenagers to make protests up on the hill and frighten them off. But somehow, I don't think that will be enough. You know what these smarty-pants clever-clogs are like. They won't be told!

So, here's where you lot come in. I want you to organise some muscle to go up to Leith Hill and smash the telescope. If anyone gets in their way, that's their lookout! None of us must be seen to be involved and none of us four must be there when it happens. We need to stay clean and invisible so we can make our dosh when the Star arrives.

Here's the plan. I need a day or so to make sure my friends in the Powers That Be are in the know and well prepared. We don't want any nosey coppers stopping our little smash- up party.

You organise the muscle, and have them meet at the foot of Leith Hill Saturday evening. I'll command the whole thing and give the start order from my luxury yacht in Poole Harbour. I have a complete super-techno control centre on my yacht." He turned to Marilyn with a Fist, and passed her what looked like a large mobile phone. "Give this to the leader of the muscle. Tell him or her in no uncertain terms not to move before they get the signal from me. I need to be sure I have the Powers That Be fully onside. I'll need to reassure the Powers that nothing will happen until Saturday midnight so there won't be people around to witness the attack. Be absolutely clear to the thugs: the go-ahead won't be given until midnight Saturday. Don't let them attack before I confirm everything. We have to keep the confidence of the Powers.

All of you, keep your heads down on Saturday night. We stay out of it for the time-being to make sure we're all around to fill our boots when the Star arrives."

Oligarch looked around the group. "Any questions?" Everyone was nodding, everyone was smiling.

"Right" concluded Oligarch. "Let's split. I've been generous enough to pay for all your coffee. Think of it as a small advance on making you all very rich. Get to work, and don't mess it up!"

As soon as the Brassers had left the café, Daksha headed back to her market stall. She knew she had to get the information to Kyle, and the rest of the SuperHeroes, with great urgency. Things were getting very serious.

CHAPTER 6. A HARBOUR RAID.

Daksha got on to Shishoom with Kyle the minute she reached her market stall. She hid behind crates of fruit and vegetables to keep things as hush-hush as possible. Before the call, Kyle had been struggling not to drop off to sleep at work. With the news from Daksha he was totally wide awake, all his senses buzzing. From Kyle, the news spread like wildfire to all the SuperHeroes. Within two hours of Daksha leaving the café, all the team had received top priority communication from Akito and Dt Wetherby-Good at the Science Centre:

"Emergency message. Shishoom for SuperHeroes lunchtime tomorrow. All must attend. Be prepared for weekend work. Extra Puma Cat guard posted tonight for Zac and Kyle. Take care. Message ends."

Zac and Kyle took extra coffee and very large food boxes with them that evening. They also armed themselves with cricket bats to frighten off trouble makers. A half a dozen Puma Cats surrounded the telescope and Grace made regular flights over the top of Leith Hill during the night.

In fact, everything remained calm, quiet and cold. Everything that is except Zac and Kyle who worked like fury. Akito had briefed them on hundreds of telescope observations he needed and, as these were made, they were transmitted to the Science Centre's giant computer. In addition, they were using the Stargazing app to make observations. Then these too were sent over for analysis.

With great event management skills, Dr Wetherby-Good had organised a giant weekend party at the Centre so nobody had any idea, that every minute, a huge mass of data was flowing into the computer, being analysed, and then spat out again. The whole Centre, including some guests from the Powers That Be, were having far too good a time to notice that.

Exhaustion really set in for Kyle and Zac as they flew home on Grace's back. In fact, Kyle nodded off to sleep and would have fallen off if Zac hadn't grabbed him by the collar.

"Nice one. Thanks mate!" said Kyle." I would have done the same for you my friend."

"Better we all stay awake" came Grace's voice. "If we all drop off to sleep, it's really game over!"

In fact, excitement kept Kyle and Zac awake at work until the big lunchtime Shishoom get together. Then both looked forward to the afternoons off they had arranged.

All the Superheroes joined the meeting on time. Akito and Dr Wetherby-Good led the discussion.

"Welcome to this meeting." Akito spoke in a grave tone, immediately commanding everyone's attention. "Have no doubt that what we are about to discuss is of the highest possible importance. We face a grave crisis. We face the biggest crisis since the beginning of mankind. The fate of all living things, perhaps the fate of the planet itself, rests on the things we decide here.

Dr Wetherby-Good will lead you through the detail. Before she does, and recognizing the seriousness of the situation, it is only right that I pay tribute to the work that has been done by the SuperHeroes over the past days. Thank you all for having worked so hard. Thank you all for having worked day and night, giving up sleep and family, to get done what needed to get done. Thank you all for putting yourselves in danger and continuing to work in the face of threats and aggression. Because of your work, huge amounts of data and observation have been processed through our mega-computer. We know so much more now.

Please recognise your achievements and give yourselves a pat on the back. Because, SuperHero team, the work is not over. In fact, it has only just begun. So please prepare yourselves for more hard work, more sleepless nights and more danger. We will triumph but there is a long upward path to climb."

"Thank you Akito." Wetherby-Good continued with the presentation. "Last time I talked to you, I listed the things we did not know about the Star from Afar. Today, I'm going to list the things we have found out, thanks to your good work.

We know the name of the group trying to oppose our efforts. They are called the Brassers. They are a gang of four. The leader is a man they call Oligarch.

They are only interested in making money. They have been very successful in the past in getting rich through other people's rubbish. They sense the Star from Afar is a big opportunity to get rich. They are well connected with the Powers That Be, and have persuaded them not to interfere with the Star, or even try to find out more about it. They will stop at nothing.

We know the Brassers will try to destroy our telescope on Leith Hill on Saturday night. We know the details. They are hiring thugs, and the whole operation will be controlled by Oligarch from his mega-yacht in Poole Harbour. We cannot let an attack happen. Our work must continue. I'll come back to this because we have to decide our action plan today. But first, more information about the object in the sky.

We now know much more about the makeup of the Star from Afar. It is absolutely not the remnants of an old star. It is not natural at all. It has been made by intelligent beings. We don't know exactly what it is made of. For that we need more data.

The Star from Afar is, in fact, two objects. The main body is a long spherical object. It looks like an inflatable airship. Think of it as about the size of the Surrey Hills. At the back of the object is a kind of control cabin. We think all the technology and information is in this control cabin. Beneath the sphere, a second, much smaller object, is attached. Probably by very strong wires. Think of it as a small gas balloon under a much bigger gas balloon. The smaller object is probably about the size of one of the barges on the River Wey.

We have studied the object's movements with great care. We know it is not simply swinging through the cosmos, being pulled this way and that by gravitational force. It is being controlled. It speeds up. It slows down. It changes course. Because of this, we can't be sure whether the object will collide with Planet Earth or simply pass by, or even when all this will happen. For this we need more data. I don't need to tell you what would happen if this object collided with our planet. It would be game over! So, I'm going to have to ask everyone to work tonight and tomorrow night. Then we'll process all the new data during Sunday and have a further

Shishoom meeting Sunday evening. By then hopefully, we'll know enough to put together an action plan to save the planet.

"First and foremost," Akito cut in, "I remind you all of the urgency of coming up with a plan to stop the Brassers and their thugs destroying our telescope on Saturday night. Without more information from the telescope, we are doomed."

There was silence among the group as they struggled to absorb the enormity of what they had heard. Heads dropped. Zac and Kyle sensed all hope of a rest disappearing.

The gloom was lifted as the calm, confident voice of Eleanor the Invisible broke the silence.

"Don't worry about the attack from the Brasser thugs. Trust me. While you were talking, I have put a plan in place. I have total confidence it will work, so you can all be confident too. We can keep on using the telescope until we have all the information we need."

– ◼ –

Wally the Walrus was taking a break from his holiday to listen to the SuperHero Shishoom call. He had taken a trip with two of his very best friends, Molly the Walrus and Solly the Walrus. He had persuaded them to visit the Scilly Isles with him. The Scillies were of course part of Wally's earlier great adventure. Wally was very popular in the Scillies and wanted to introduce Molly and Solly to his friends as well as to the wonderful seafood that could be found in the bays and harbours. So, they took a leisurely, calm swim from the Arctic to the Isles, stopping in on Ireland on the way.

All was calm on the Scillies. In fact, very few people had even heard of the Star from Afar. But Wally wanted to keep up with developments, so he joined the Shishoom call. Halfway through the call, Wally received a text message from his great friend Eleanor. It read: -

"Wally, let's you and I have a quick, separate conversation while the others are talking. I have an idea!"

Wally was delighted by the invitation and spent the next ten minutes in deep conversation, making plans with his close friend. They concluded the call with full agreement. The hair on Wally's tusks bristled with excitement. He had to move quickly. His first job was to find Molly and Solly and get them in on the act. The search was short. He found his friends exactly where he thought they would be: munching seafood from the harbour rocks. Wally explained the situation and went through the full background. Molly and Solly could not wait to get started!

Now they needed a sea captain and a powerful boat. After careful thought, Wally decided to approach the red-faced man. The very same man who had given him such a hard time for sleeping on his boat during Wally's last trip. The red-faced man was not always easy to deal with but Wally felt he might just have the toughness and determination they needed. They found their man on his ice cream stand, looking a little glum. With the falling temperatures, ice cream sales had practically disappeared. "Bloomin melted away!" the red-faced man shouted. "Bloomin melted away!"

Wally told the red-faced man the plan hatched up with Eleanor. He was careful to tell the whole story including the dangers that lay ahead.

"I can't wait to get started!" cried the man, the moment Wally finished his tale. "It's got to be better than trying to sell ice-creams to people who are already bloomin half frozen! I need a little time to get ready and prepared. Meet me at my boat in one hour. We are going to have fun!"

The red-faced man would like to have made the journey at warp-speed. His boat was very powerful and he wanted to show it off. Wally persuaded him that calm and caution were better ideas.

"We absolutely do not want to draw attention to ourselves as we travel. There are spies in many places. Let's take it easy. As long as we arrive in Poole harbour by Saturday afternoon, all will be well."

As it turned out, the journey proved leisurely and relaxed. The weather was calm, cold and clear. The red-faced man loved piloting his flashy boat. And things for the Walruses could not have been better. Red-faced man had brought along sacks of shell-fish. All Wally, Solly and Molly had to do was enjoy the cruise, eat and sleep.

– ■ –

For Eleanor, things were much less relaxing. She began to feel the pressure of being at the centre of the plan to stop the Brassers' thugs attacking the telescope on Saturday night. The plan had lots of different elements, lots of moving pieces. Eleanor began to wonder if she had been too confident with the other SuperHeroes. There was so much at stake here and so much danger. To calm everyone's anxiety, she set up a system of regular contact with all those involved.

It was clear that the Wally's boat was making good steady progress through Friday night.

Then early Saturday morning, Grace let Eleanor know that she had Zac and Kyle on board. They were very tired but a good night's work had been completed. Still much to do, but progress had been made with no interruptions.

By Saturday mid-afternoon, the red-faced man had piloted his boat into Poole Harbour. He and his three Walrus passengers were busy scanning the Marina for Oligarch's mega-yacht, and also keeping their eyes peeled for first sightings of Puma Cats.

After the good news, bad news started to come in.

The thugs hired by the Brassers had started to appear in Abinger Hammer, Peaslake and Ewhurst. There were plenty of them and they were muscled and well-armed. Walking sticks with points, cricket bats and stout branches chopped from trees were in evidence. The thugs were noisy and aggressive and soon begun to upset local residents, shopkeepers and publicans. The local constabulary had clearly been briefed by the Powers to leave well alone.

Eleanor became really concerned about what would happen if Oligarch gave an early signal for the mob to attack the telescope.

She had been told that the thugs were to start massing at Abinger between the hours of eight and nine but that the go-ahead signal from Oligarch wouldn't come until midnight. The tension was rising! Time was ticking by.

Early evening, Grace Shishoomed in to say she was returning to the Hill with Zac and Kyle. They had flown over the gangs of thugs and the very sight of them had turned the SuperHeroes pale. Was Eleanor absolutely sure that the night's work on the telescope should go ahead?

"We, the SuperHeroes will prevail!" came back the response. Though in truth Eleanor sounded a lot more confident than she felt. The danger to which Zac and Kyle was exposed was huge. The danger to the planet of course was even greater.

At seven o'clock, Eleanor got the news that the Walruses had located the Oligarch's magnificent boat, and that all three Walruses were now in the water. The chief concern expressed by Wally and his friends was that they might be in the water several hours without food! The red-faced man told them in clear terms that eating was not as important as saving the planet. So, Wally, Solly and Molly were now circling around within ten minutes swim of the Superyacht.

The Puma Cats reported that all the Brasser thugs were now moving towards Abinger. A mass of litter and a lot of noise accompanied them. The residents of Abinger had every window boarded up, every gate and door locked. The atmosphere was thick with menace.

– ■ –

About nine o'clock, the light began to fade around the Poole Marina. It was then that the first Puma Cat appeared in plain sight on the Harbour Wall. Half an hour later, there were four magnificent cats parading along the wall, right outside Oligarch's yacht.

On board the yacht, Oligarch was too busy wining and dining his companion Marilyn with a Fist to take notice of what was happening on the Marina wall. He needed to get supper over and then make his call to the leader of the thugs. If he didn't call by midnight, they would all go home and he would have to pay them anyway. Oligarch was preoccupied, so Marilyn was the first to notice the Puma Cats.

"Look, oh do look!" she cried, "What enormous, beautiful, graceful creatures! They must be worth an absolute fortune!"

It was the words "absolute fortune" that got Oligarch's attention. Oligarch looked out of the enormous cabin window at the sensational cats.

"Right." he said to Marilyn "Let's get down the gangplank and see what's happening. I sense that there's business to be done here."

The conversation on the Harbour wall could not have gone better. The Oligarch and Marilyn were charming and entertaining. The Puma Cats purred with delight at the interest they were being shown. The Puma Cats told a very interesting (and very well-rehearsed!) story. It went something like this:

Puma Cats were the rarest and most valuable cats on the planet. They were only bred in Surrey and from there, they were shipped all over the world. A single Puma Cat was worth a half a million pounds. The four Cats that Oligarch and Marilyn had met were part of a group of ten that was to be shipped by boat to a very rich Sheik in the Middle East. But they had escaped and were in desperate need of kind people to help them. The four Cats with whom they were talking had been sent out as scouts, looking for nice kind people.

"Ourrr frrrinends arrre so hungrrry and lonely." said one of the Puma Cats. "Might we take you to them? If you could help us in any small way, we would be so grrrrateful!"

Oligarch couldn't believe his luck. He took Marilyn aside, and whispered in her ear. "This is money for old rope – or old moggie cats!" he said. "We'll follow this lot, then capture all ten of the little critters. We'll throw them in a cage, and we'll flog them to some poor mug for five million smackers. Not bad for an evening's work.

There's nobody on the boat, so I'll nip in and lock the doors and hatch covers. Then hey ho and off we go! We'll be back before midnight five million quid richer and ready to let all hell loose on Leith Hill."

In fact, there had been five cats on the Harbour wall, not just the four that Oligarch and Marilyn were talking with. And just as soon as the four Puma Cats led the Brassers off to meet the other escaped Cats, the fifth Puma Cat emerged from her hiding place. She walked along the harbour wall, right at the edge. She was careful to flash her emerald eyes out over the water. The message was sent, and received by the three very hungry Walruses.

- ■ -

At Abinger, things were kicking off in a big way as more and more thugs arrived. The shouting turned to screaming. Fights broke out among different thug factions. Tempers were lost. Noses and arms were broken. Several times the thug leader had to shout for calm.

"We can't go up the Hill until we get the word from Oligarch!" he cried." That won't come until midnight. Save the fighting for when we get to the telescope."

Zac and Kyle could hear the noise of the chaos from up on top of the Hill. They told each other not to be afraid. they had to work. They had to get through the night. Secretly, both wondered if they would see the dawn.

- ■ -

Down in Poole Harbour, Wally, Molly and Solly reached the mega-yacht quickly and quietly. They held a brief conversation with the Puma cat.

"Look," she purred "there's nobody on the boat. Oligarch and Marilyn are off on a Puma Cat visiting trip. I will stand guard, and I rrreckon you have about an hour to get the job done. Unfortunately, Oligarch has locked all the doors and hatch coverrrs."

"Don't worry about that," replied Wally. "We can do what we need to do right at the top of the boat. They won't even know we've been here until of course they try to work in their super-techno control room!"

Getting on to the boat was the first challenge. When you have heavy heads and heavy tusks like Wally and his pals, clambering up on to a big shiny boat was not the easiest. But with huge effort, much grunting and groaning and constant complaining of hunger, they made it.

They now had two more levels to climb before they reached the top of the boat. The process was repeated, the hunger got worse.

Finally, all three were right at the top of the boat. Here they found as expected lots of cables and wires, linking together all sorts of techno-looking boxes, objects and antennae fastened to the deck.

"Right." said Wally. "This is where we do the famous Walrus Roll. We all lie down next to each other, tusks facing the prow. The on the count of three, we all roll three times to starboard. Then on the next count, we go three rolls to port. We continue that until the deck is nice and clear and flat. Time is a-ticking, so let's get this done. One, two, three! Do the Walrus Roll!"

The Walruses were beautifully co-ordinated, a real dance team. Every time they rolled, wires snapped, cables were ripped out and techno boxes were crushed. After fifteen minutes, the deck was covered with broken bits and pieces, with no semblance of order.

A call came from Puma Cat. "Times overrr. Back in the harbourrrr!"

There were there big splashes as Wally, Solly and Molly did beautifully co- ordinated dive bombs in to the water. Then silence as they swam underwater back to the red-faced man's boat, hoping that a seafood meal awaited them.

– ■ –

As the time ticked toward midnight, things got worse in Abinger. Out of frustration and anger, two small groups of thugs decided to force their way up the Hill in advance of Oligarch's go-ahead. An emergency call was made to Eleanor. The thugs were successfully driven back by a fire-breathing Dragon swooping down the Hill!

The tension mounted for the SuperHeroes and particularly for Eleanor. If the whole mob didn't wait for word from Oligarch and mayhem broke loose, it would be curtains for the telescope, the SuperHeroes working on it and the future of the planet.

– ■ –

The angry mood of the mob was matched by the frustration of Oligarch and Marilyn. They had walked for miles around the Harbour following the Puma Cats. Up this road and back down the other. Out on this jetty and then back down again. Right round this roundabout, up this dark alley, round the back of this building and then back to the roundabout.

Every time they shouted at the Puma Cats, they got the same reply. "You will see Puma Cats very soon. They are hiding, because they arrre verrry valuable."

They reached a part of the harbour wall where they could see back to where the Oligarch's yacht was anchored. They were a long way away and it was less than thirty minutes before midnight.

"Right," said Oligarch to Marilyn. "We're being had for fools here. Let's grab these four critters, drag them back to the boat and lock them up. Forget the others!"

Oligarch turned around to grab a Puma Cat tail. Nothing. They were all gone. Disappeared into thin air. Not a Puma Cat in sight. Not a single whisker.

"We've been had!" screamed Oligarch. "Fast as we can, back to the yacht, before the rest of the night gets botched!"

Oligarch enjoyed life and wasn't in the best condition for running. So Marilyn had to half drag, half carry him back. At one stage she thought the rushing, and stress and anger would be the end of Oligarch. To be honest she was in two minds whether this would be a good or a bad thing! Eventually, panting and groaning, they made it back to the yacht at six minutes to midnight.

Oligarch made a quick inspection of the doors and hatch covers. "Thank goodness!" he cried hoarsely. "They're all still locked and secured. Nobody has been interfering with them! Right, I'll go straight down to the super-techno control room and contact the boss of the thugs. I'll give the word to let them all loose on the telescope and anybody who's guarding it. This is going to be fun!

Marilyn, you just check the upper decks and then we'll get together when all the work is done. We'll have a nice glass of celebratory English bubbly. No time to lose!"

Oligarch undid the locks and got down to his control centre without problem. There gleaming in front of him was his precious control centre. His pride and joy. He could make secret contact with any part of the planet with his favourite toy. Now to unleash the chaos on Leith Hill! He went to the master switch for the equipment. He turned it on. Nothing! The screens remained blank. A moment of panic crossed Oligarch's mind. Only a few minutes left. He turned the master switch off, then on again. Nothing! He checked the lighting and the heating in the boat. They were working fine. It was just his techno communication centre. He couldn't get to the outside world. He was alone. Isolated. Without the call, there would be no attack on Leith Hill. He would have to pay those villains anyway. He had been fooled by a bunch of Puma Cats. It was the worst night of his life. He lay on the floor. Like a spoiled child, he kicked and thrashed. He flailed his arm against a table leg. He smashed the glass face of his huge bling-bling designer watch. He screamed long and hard!

Marilyn came through the door. She looked down on Oligarch, part in concern, part in pity.

"Someone has wrecked my techno centre," he cried. "I can't communicate with those stupid thugs. All is lost!"

"If you want to know what's happened, come and see the top deck. All the aerials, all the communication wires, all the satellite dishes are gone. Wrecked. You locked the inside of the boat, but you forgot that without the kit on the top deck, your wonderful techno centre is useless. Someone has made us look very stupid this evening!"

"Someone will pay for this. This is war." screamed Oligarch. "I'm not finished yet!"

– ■ –

At Abinger, the noise and chaos increased the closer the clock got to midnight.

The boss of the thugs saw the tension and the fighting increase. He realised that the later it got, the less the chance there was of a call from the Oligarch. He had a plan.

It was 30 seconds after midnight. The thugs were ready to go! He couldn't control them for much longer and he dare not release them without the Oligarch's call. The thug boss had to make a decision. He had a microphone with him. He picked it up, and made himself heard above the noise.

"Calm down everyone. The attack on the telescope is postponed. I repeat the attack on the telescope is postponed. You will be paid in full for this evening. You must go to your homes quietly, and you will find your cash waiting for you. There will be more chances to earn dosh. But if you create problems, you won't be paid, and there won't be other chances. Thank you and good night to you all."

Fortunately, the thought of ready cash waiting at home did the trick. The thugs left, muttering their frustration to each other. In thirty minutes, the area was clear.

Zac and Kyle could hear all the hub-bub at the top of the Hill. They were hugely relieved when they heard the megaphone announcement. To celebrate the departure of the thugs, they took an extra coffee break with very yummy biscuits.

"Lush that those noisy thugs have gone," said Kyle.

"Lush is the word," said Zac. "Now we can work in peace!"

– ■ –

At last Eleanor could relax. Her plan had worked. All the SuperHeroes had delivered. The work on the Star from Afar could continue. Somewhere, at the back of her mind however, there was a warning voice. The work on understanding the Star and fighting off the Brassers was far, far from over.

CHAPTER 7. BIG MEETINGS. BIG DECISIONS.

After the shenanigans at Poole Harbour and Leith Hill on Saturday, rumours and gossip around the Star from Afar ran wild. Everybody who was anybody in the Surrey Hills was talking about what was and what wasn't going on. Secrecy was no longer possible.

So, not surprisingly, all the SuperHeroes, plus Dr Wetherby-Good and Akito joined the Sunday Shishoom conference ahead of time.

"This is a landmark conference," Akito kicked off. "We have learned much over the weekend. However, I don't want to get your expectations up too high. It seems the task in front of us is, if anything, tougher than ever.

Dr Wetherby-Good will fill you in on the details we have learned. Before she does though, I have a few background things to report.

Firstly, everyone in the Surrey Hills and of course everyone here, applauds the bravery and courage shown by those who worked so hard in the face of the planned attack on the telescope at Leith Hill. I must mention in particular Kyle and Zac, Wally the Walrus and his friends Solly and Molly, all the Puma Cats, the generous man from the Scillies who gave enormous help to Wally and his pals and of course Eleanor the Invisible who masterminded the whole event. Thank you for your courage and commitment. You have done the Surrey Hills proud!"

The applause and cheers lasted more than two minutes. Then Akito resumed.

"The degree to which we outwitted and foiled the Brassers is very clear. I have already been contacted by Oligarch, their leader. He is a threatening and unpleasant man and he has become desperate. In fact, he has offered a top of the line huge bling-bling designer watch to all the SuperHeroes if we stop our activity now. I point – blank refused of course. He then simply threatened to wipe us out."

"Maybe" chimed in Kyle quietly, "maybe we could just see the huge bling-bling designer watch before we decide. They are such lush watches..."

"No, no, no!" roared the other SuperHeroes.

"Well okay, but maybe I could have one just for the weekend?"

"No, "roared the SuperHeroes. "Not even for a minute."

Kyle finally took the point and Akito continued.

"As you all know, there is now little secrecy left around the so-called Star from Afar. The Powers That Be are fully aware of what's going on. I have told them of everything we have found out. It's annoying and frustrating but they continue to sit on the fence. They won't stop anything we want to do. Neither will they stop any of the Brassers' activities. They keep saying "Let's wait and see." As you will realise when you have heard from Dr Wetherby-Good, this is totally unrealistic. But on the other hand, a way forward is not obvious.

So, I will now hand over to Dr Wetherby-Good who has analysed all the new data that has come in. Be prepared for a tough discussion."

"We can now one hundred per cent confirm that the object in space has been made by intelligent beings. The shape and size of both objects is as I described them last time. The material used to make the objects is very interesting. It is, in fact, what we call Goldbeaters Skin. This is a very tough natural material. It is the treated membrane of the intestines of cattle. On Planet Earth we have used this in the past for separating the leaves of metal in gold beating. On Earth it has also been used to make large inflatable balloons.

Thousands and thousands of these membranes have been fixed together to hold the contents inside both the larger and smaller objects.

"And what do these objects contain?" asked Ariadne.

"They contain masses and masses of rubbish!" replied the good doctor.

"Everything. Old household waste. Old cars. Old furniture. Everything no longer wanted in the place where these objects started. It's like the biggest rubbish tip on Planet Earth flying round space looking for a way of getting rid of the problem. Now, before you get all angry and bent out of shape about someone's rubbish flying around space, we have an immediate problem to discuss.

We now know the objects are being controlled from another planet, probably in another galaxy. The larger object has rocket motors. They can slow the object down, speed the object up or change course. There is a command centre on the larger object. We think that centre is run by robots. We don't think there are living creatures aboard but we are not sure. We are sure that the command centre is receiving orders and commands from the home planet. But we can't read them. We are too far away from the Star from Afar."

"So, get to the point, please." called out the Green Man. "Is this flying pile of junk going to hit us or not?"

"Excellent question," Wetherby- Good came straight back. "If their command centre wants the objects to hit Planet Earth, that is what they will do. They can alternatively use their rocket motors to voyage around Planet Earth and go elsewhere."

"How long have we got to find out?" came Vesta's voice.

"Until the end of this week. By then the objects will be at their closest point to Planet Earth. Then its hit or miss!"

"What are the wonderful Powers That Be doing?" rasped the usually calm Grace.

"They will do nothing until we find out what the messages from the home planet to the Star say."

"And can we do that? And how do we do it?" This was Zac, ever practical.

"Oh yes," said Dr Wetherby-Good. "It can be done. We have the technology to intercept the messages as they come in. We can even access previous messages. But to do so, we will have to place one of our transmitter-receivers on the object in space!"

Suddenly, the meeting was totally silent. Even the Montmorencies stopped squabbling in the background. It seemed like the silence lasted forever.

Then, the small, calm, influential voice of Eleanor the Invisible. "So, let's get it done. Let's choose to journey to the object in space, to the famous Star from Afar."

The meeting went wild. Everyone was talking, shouting, arm waving, all at the same time. There was an explosion of "WHO'S?" and "HOW'S?"and "WHAT'S?" and "WHEN'S?" and "ARE YOU KIDDING?" and "DON'T ASK ME?" Fear and doubt filled the air.

"Okay, SuperHeroes. Pipe down the lot of you. Do you think they got the first man on the Moon by shouting, and screaming and creating a big bazaar of noise and confusion?" It was Eleanor's calm, authoritative voice again. "We've come a long way. Now we've got little time left to save the planet. Let's focus on the task in hand. Let's have one question per person. And we don't move on until we have an action plan to deal with each question."

"I'll kick off with a question to my friend Akito," said Dr Wetherby-Good. "If we are to be successful in getting a transmitter on the Star from Afar, when does it have to be done?"

"I've been calculating while you have been talking," replied Akito. "Given the relative positions of the object, the Earth and the Moon, and of course the weather forecast, the only time we can make a launch is this Wednesday at thirty minutes past midday. There are no other options. I know time is short. The good news is that I can have the transmitter-receiver ready by then."

Vesta jumped in. "Is it going to be possible to get a transmitter on the object without sending someone along with it?"

"There is no question of doing this without someone going into space. The technical difficulties are far too great for this to be done remotely." Wetherby-Good replied.

There was a long silence as the group took in the implications of what was being said.

Finally. "Who will go?" this was Wally the Walrus, thinking about the difficulty of getting his tusks into a space helmet and of course about going without seafood for a long spaceflight.

"I would like you to choose me to go." The calm voice of Eleanor again. "Ever since the magicians created my magic gloves and cape that allow me to fly around the planet, I have dreamed of going into space. To experience the wonder of the universe. To see our Blue Planet from afar. Now, I have a chance to do just that and maybe help save the Blue Planet by succeeding in the mission.

I know I will need more power to get into space. My cape and gloves are not powerful enough to escape the Earth's gravity. I also know that I will need a special suit to survive in space. I have some ideas and I'm hoping others will help."

Again, a long silence, eventually broken by Zac. "Can we get a space rocket from the Powers That Be?"

"Sadly, out of the question," Akito came back. "The Powers will remain undecided bunglers. They won't stop us going into space but they won't help."

Amy Elizabeth contributed in her usual precise way. "Dear Green Man," she said. "You were very helpful in getting your magician friends to make the gloves and cape that power Eleanor's flights around the planet. Do you think you can be of help again?"

"I've been thinking about this a great deal," Green Man's gruff voice came back. "My best contribution to this effort is to make an apparatus that will allow Eleanor to escape the Earth's gravity. I have something in mind. The power of traditional longbows is extraordinary. There is a history of making and using these bows in the Surrey Hills. They are made of yew which also grows locally. I'm thinking of making a monster yew longbow with my friends in the forest. We will then be able to fire Eleanor into space like an arrow. Once Eleanor gets speed and height from the longbow lift off, she will be able to use her new cape and gloves to manoeuvre in space. The cape and gloves of course have to be new, much more powerful than the current ones.

The best use of my time is to construct the longbow and I think I can be ready by Wednesday. But if I do this, I won't be able to organise Eleanor's new cape, gloves and space suit."

"Before we go on, we should ask Eleanor how she feels about being shot into space from a longbow, like an arrrrow?" This from one of the Puma Cats.

"Well," said Eleanor, "this is going to be one scary step for a daughter of a Surrey Hills woodcutter, and one giant step for the planet! That's how I feel. I am scared and excited at the same time. But it's a privilege to help getting this job done."

"How would the rest of you feel," asked Ariadne, if I worked with the magicians on new gloves, cape and a space suit?" In truth, Ariadne fancied the idea of being a fashion designer, so she was grateful when everyone nodded agreement.

"What about the Brassers. Are they going to leave us alone?" asked Kyle hopefully.

"From what I hear, not a chance." The reply came from Fred Goodfellow. "Rumour has it that the Brassers are madder than ever by what happened at Poole Harbour and Leith Hill. Plus, they know now that the Star from Afar is probably full of rubbish. To the Brassers, rubbish means money, loot, dosh. That's all they care about. They think the Star hitting the Earth is the best idea since sliced bread. They think they will make fortunes. So, they will be determined to cut off any efforts we make to stop a disaster.

And if I can make some suggestions to try and keep us safe. Let's move our planned space launch site away from Leith Hill where we have the telescope. At first, I thought of Box Hill which has the advantage of being very high. But it also very well known. So, I have spied out an area known as Hill Top Barn, near East Clandon. There's a large open space, though relatively well hidden from the road. We can use that as our launch site. We will leave the telescope at Leith Hill and keep some of the Puma Cats patrolling there. Hopefully, this will fool the Brassers and get us twenty-four hours of quiet.

Meantime, Kyle, Zac and I can try and recruit some muscle of our own. The word is out about the danger to the planet so there may be many good folks from the Hills ready to defend our efforts."

Kyle chipped in. "I think this planning is absolutely ace," he said. "I have got know you SuperHeroes, and I think together we can do anything. My only point is, can't we have a huge bling-bling designer watch just for a little while, it would really help me....?"

"NOOOOOO!!" The roars of the SuperHeroes drowned out the rest of Kyle's plea.

Dr Wetherby-Good brought the meeting back to order. "Look, we have masses to do, and very little time to do it. I'm going to suggest that we don't waste any more time in meeting and discussion. I suggest we appoint Vesta, Goddess of Fire, as coordinator. If you run into problems, get in touch with the Goddess. Otherwise, push forward on your projects at top speed. It is clear, failure is not an option. So, unless we talk in the meantime, we'll all meet at Hill Top Barn at eleven on Wednesday morning, to prepare for the big lift -off.

The SuperHeroes started their tasks immediately and worked harder than ever. Ariadne got in touch with the magicians who had created Eleanor's original flying suit. The Goddess explained the plans and the magicians came up with marvellous solutions. They worked everything in Goldbeaters Skin, the same tough, flexible material that the Star from Afar was made from. They created a space suit to keep Eleanor safe. Effectively, it was an overall, which covered all of Eleanor's body except her head. The extraordinary thing about the design was that there were two layers of material. The space between the layers would be filled with water. Water, of course, was Eleanor's friend; it protected her from all danger. Exactly what she needed on a long space flight.

The cape and the gloves were completely remade to give them turbo super power. The cape would now come down to Eleanor's feet. It was heavy with many folds. The gloves were much bigger than before and gloves and cape together would give her the power she needed for space flight. The boots were also redesigned. Eleanor would not be working in the fields of the planet. She would be flying in space! So, her new boots were lighter and more flexible. They were super-cool designer space-trainers! Finally, the helmet. A truly amazing construction. It had tubes on either side to link to Eleanor's oxygen pack on her back. And it had a long, pointy shape, to ensure maximum speed at take off!

In all honesty, it was not the technical designs that interested Ariadne the most. It was the colours. You see, Ariadne was at heart an artist. In another life, she would have been a great fashion designer. So, everything was created in the same colours. Ariadne chose a mottle of green and blue. The blue because of Eleanor's affinity with water but also because of Ariadne's love of the Mediterranean. The green because of the forests and meadows of the Surrey Hills, an important part of the planet that the SuperHeroes were trying to save.

All was finished late Tuesday night. Ariadne asked the magicians for one last fitting, with her as the model.

"Ariadne, we are sure all the clothing will fit," said the head designer of the magician team. "We have taken all the measurements with great care. Eleanor will be delighted."

"Oh, please," said Ariadne, "it's always better to be safe than sorry. I am exactly the same size as Eleanor, so it will be a good test."

The magicians suspected that there was more to Ariadne's request than "one final check." However they agreed that Ariadne should try on the outfit which she did with remarkable speed.

The effect was stunning. Everything in the wonderful blue-green mottle. Space-trainers just visible below the magnificent cape. The overalls fitting well, with the blue-green colour of the outer skin ensuring that the water would not make Eleanor completely invisible. The gloves, almost like giant claws, gave her a formidable appearance. And the helmet, with its long point, adding a half a metre to her height.

"If Eleanor gets to meet anyone in space, they will be truly impressed!" said Ariadne." You have all done a remarkable job. But do you think it would be a good idea if I borrowed the outfit for just one evening? I could test it out in town, and see what kind of reaction I get."

The horrified looks on the faces of all the magicians gave Ariadne her answer. "I guess it was worth a try," she said in a disappointed voice.

CHAPTER EIGHT. FIGHT AND FLIGHT.

Across at Hill Top Barn in East Clandon, the Green Man had assembled a large number of his friends and people who worked in the forests of the Surrey Hills.

"Right, good people," he started "The reason we are all here today is a matter of great importance."

He felt a tug on his sleeve. It was Amy Elizabeth, trying to get his attention.

"What do you want, Amy Elizabeth?" he said, "Can't you see I'm busy?"

"They're not listening," she said. "None of them are listening."

"But it's a very important thing," said the Green Man. "Its all about the future of the planet!"

"They're not listening because they just want to look at the amazing view and enjoy the sight and smell of all these gorgeous flowers."

"So, what do we do?" said the Green Man, now in super-grumpy mood. "Let a giant pile of rubbish hit our beautiful planet?"

"No, here's what we do," said Amy Elizabeth with great authority, "Claire who works on growing the flowers on this land will give a short talk on the flowers growing on this lovely piece of land and how she supplies them to people in the neighbourhood. I'll chip in with a few words on the view. Once your friends know what they are looking at, you will get their undivided attention."

So that's what they did. Amy Elizabeth talked about the stunning views to the north, right across the valley of the River Wey. She pointed out the high towers of Woking, admired by some, not so loved by others. Then Claire explained the sustainable methods used to grow the beautiful flowers in the heart of the Surrey Hills. She called her activity PlantPassion, and supplied many people in the Surrey Hills with wonderful locally grown blooms.

This and the answer to a few questions did the trick. The Green Man could now get his team organised. The Green Man explained the whole story of the Star from Afar to the team. He concluded with "So now all we have to do is get Eleanor the Invisible into space."

"Is that all?" shouted one of the forest workers. "You make it sound a lot easier than growing flowers in the Surrey Hills."

"What we are going to do is build a huge yew longbow and fire Eleanor into space like an arrow. The longbow will be secured horizontal to the ground. To get enough power, we need a bow with a stave thirty meters long. So, I need you all to scour the forests for yew staves seasoned for at least six months. We need hundreds of them so the magicians of the forest and I can bind them all together. We will use a magical form of lamination so the stave will be enormously strong and flexible. So, search the forests, all the timber yards, all the carpenters who work with yew and explain to them the importance of what we are doing."

"I know a couple of longbow specialists who still make bows by hand." This from a woman in the crowd.

"Great news," said the Green Man "Get on to them, and get as much seasoned yew as they can spare. And remember, time is of the essence!"

As the Green Man's team split up to search the region for yew staves, the two young dinosaurs, Montmorency the second and Montmorency the third, came wandering up the stony path to Hill Top Barn. The usual bickering was going on. Montmorency the third had just "accidentally" trodden on Montmorency the second's foot. In revenge, Montmorency the second was twisting his brother's tail. The hub-bub attracted a crowd from the Green Man's team, interested to see who would win this battle of brotherly love.

The Green Man stepped in. "Stop all this nonsense, young dinosaurs! You are distracting my team. I have enough hard work for you two boyos to tire you out for the whole day. No need for your silly games!"

The Green Man led the Dinosaurs down to the main meadow at Hill Top Barn. It was huge, mainly flat, covered in grass and had uninterrupted views to the north. Behind the meadow was a dense forest.

"Okay, my young friends. This is where we will launch Eleanor into space. We will launch her to the north where there are no obstacles immediately in her path.

We will need to tilt the longbow up towards the sky. So, the middle of the stave of the bow needs to be eight metres above the ground, supported by two oak posts. The oak posts will take a huge strain when we fire the bow, so deep foundations are needed.

Behind the longbow, the ground needs excavating so that we can get the launch angle exactly right. The boffins at the Science Centre say the launch angle has to be precise for a successful lift-off. So, there is a lot of digging to do!"

Montmorency the second interrupted. "Oh please, Mr Green Man, can we two do all the digging? I'll soon show you how I can dig much better than my lazy layabout brother."

"You're on," replied the Green Man. "I'll get the nice flower lady to decide who's best. I am sure she will award a beautiful bouquet to the winner."

The digging had started before the Green Man had finished speaking. "There are some big stones and boulders to dig out," said Montmorency the third. "What shall do with them?"

"Put them in a pile at the top of the field at the edge of the forest," said the Green Man. "We might find a use for them for them later."

– ■ –

While the digging and the space-suit designing was moving forward, Zac, Kyle and Fred Goodfellow were on a mission to recruit people to help ensure the launch into space would take place.

The Brassers were the biggest threat to the launch. The potential danger from the Star from Afar and whether it would hit planet Earth was out in the open. Everybody had an opinion. It was clear from all the rumours that, after their disasters at Poole Harbour and Leith Hill, the Brassers were more determined than ever to stop SuperHero activity to save the planet. The Powers That Be stayed sitting on the fence. They would not stop the SuperHeroes but they wouldn't protect them from the Brassers either. So, the SuperHeroes would have to protect themselves and in particular they would have to protect their space launch. For the moment, thanks to the clever plans of Farmer Goodfellow, the location of the launch site was still a closely kept secret. But everyone knew it was only matter of time before the Brassers found out. They would then for sure organise thugs to storm the launch site and stop the lift-off.

So, Kyle, Zac and Farmer Goodfellow launched "STAND UP TO THE BULLIES AND SAVE OUR PLANET." They formed a team of friends and made speeches in the town centres of Farnham, Godalming, Guildford, Reigate, Dorking, Hazelmere, Cranleigh, Leatherhead, Woking, Camberley and Epsom as well as in a dozen classic Surrey villages. They visited pubs, coffee bars, sports clubs and outdoor learning centres all across the Surrey Hills.

 At all their meetings, the opening words were always the same.

136

"Our planet is under huge threat. That you know. That you can see by looking at the object called the Star from Afar getting ever closer. We are Surrey Hills SuperHeroes seeking one thing. Knowledge that will prevent the Star from harming the planet.

There is a group who opposes our plan to find out more. They are called the Brassers and think the Star from Afar will bring them wealth, so they want no interference. We need your help to resist them. The work will be tough and dangerous. we need you to commit to helping us this Tuesday night and Wednesday morning. We cannot tell you where yet because we don't want the Brassers to find out. We will provide a hard hat. Please bring strong boots and gloves, and cricket bats or walking sticks. Midnight on Tuesday we will Shishoom you the location details."

By late Tuesday evening, a SuperHero support army of five hundred brave volunteers had been recruited.

"Do you think we have recruited enough people?" Kyle asked the others after a presentation to a local rugby club on Tuesday evening.

"I'll give you the answer to that question this time tomorrow" answered Zac. "Meantime I can tell you that I don't know what effect our volunteers will have on the Brasser thugs, but they sure scare me!"

"By the way," said Kyle, "I have figured a way of telling the Brasser spies among the groups we talk to."

"And what's that, Mr Spymaster?" Said Zac.

"The Brasser spies all have really nice huge bling-bling designer watches. I'm almost tempted to join them and get one myself."

– ■ –

Activity at Hill Top Barn continued all night. The area had been patrolled continuously by a combination of volunteers and Puma Cats. There was no sign of trouble and everyone assumed the location was still a secret. By early morning, the Dinosaurs had dug out the post-holes and the giant oak posts were installed. They were now scraping out the earth behind where the longbow would be positioned. Competitive as ever, each brother believed he was a better digger than the other. Each repeatedly asked the Puma Cats and volunteers for confirmation of their superiority.

The Green Man and his team of forest helpers had made great progress in binding and lashing the ash staves together. They now had a flexible, strong stave of just over thirty metres in length. Just after six in the morning, the magicians arrived with a mighty bow string and the retaining ropes that would hold the bow string once it had been pulled back to its limit. When the retaining ropes were cut at exactly thirty minutes past midday, the immense power of the bow would be released and Eleanor fired into space.

The next arrivals were much less welcome. By 6.30, a few Brasser thugs started to walk up the hill towards Hill Top Barn.

"The first of our Brasser friends have arrived," Kyle communicated to Farmer Goodfellow who was in the Barn control room. "I figure this means that they found out the location about an hour ago. For the moment, we'll keep them out of the Hill Top Barn area. But more are certain to arrive, so I'm looking forward to seeing more of our volunteers. Meantime, I'm seriously thinking about bashing one of the thugs on the head and stealing their huge bling-bling designer watch. Over and out!"

The tension mounted throughout the morning, inside and outside the site. The SuperHeroes knew they had to make the space launch by thirty minutes after midday. Eleanor knew she had to be in her spacesuit and positioned like an arrow on the bow string well before lift-off. The Green Man had a million technical details to deal with. The Brassers knew they had to stop the launch or their dreams of wealth would be gone. And the SuperHeroes with their volunteers had to stop the Brassers.

Ariadne and Eleanor were in deep conversation as they rode the Fjord horses up the stony lane towards Hill Top Barn. At the entry gate, they were jeered by a few Brasser thugs.

"YOU'LL NEVER MAKE IT!"

"YOU ARE USELESS DO-GOODERS STOPPING US MAKING MONEY!"

"THE STAR FROM AFAR IS OUR RIGHT!"

The chants were intimidating. There was no violence, but menace was in the air. SuperHero volunteers at the gate got Ariadne and Eleanor through safely, and held back the thugs from gaining entry.

"I know how scary this must be for you," Ariadne said to Eleanor. "I will help you into your magnificent space suit of which, if I'm honest, I am very jealous. I will stay with you until lift off. I will help you on to the small wooden sled that the Green Man has made. The end of the sled has a notch which fits on the bow string. When the retaining ropes are cut, the sled will accelerate across the short ash runway which crosses over to the stave of the bow, and you will be launched into space like an arrow."

They dismounted from their horses inside the barn where Eleanor would put on her spacesuit.

"To be honest Ariadne," Eleanor replied in calm tones," I am excited about going into space. In fact, I think I prefer the idea of space travel then facing those Brasser Thugs.

The one thing I am a little nervous about is navigating in space. The boffins tell me I should be just over 48 hours in space in total. It's going to take me 24 hours to reach my objective and I will have the transmitter-receiver on the outward journey to help me navigate. Once I have secured the transmitter-receiver, I will be out of contact and on my own. I do want to get back home again and celebrate saving the Planet with the SuperHeroes. "

Ariadne put down her backpack and drew out an intriguing scientific instrument, beautifully crafted in brass.

"This is an Astrolabe. I have used this for over two thousand years in all of my travels. It is an amazing device that helps identify heavenly bodies. For hundreds of years, Astrolabes have helped sailors and travellers navigate by reference to the stars. It will help you return from the Star from Afar. Please take it. I do want you to return safely if only so I can borrow your amazing space suit!"

For a moment Eleanor was overcome by emotion. Then reality stepped in. She had a short time to get ready for lift off.

Three hours before lift-off, nearly all the five hundred SuperHero volunteers had arrived. Zac addressed them and the Puma Cats. Both groups would be key in protecting the launch.

"Firstly welcome. We have an essential task we all know will be tough. You will have seen the Brasser thugs as you arrived. Many more will come. They are not a pleasant bunch. They must not be allowed to destroy our space launch.

I am dividing the volunteers into four groups. I want the toughest of you to control the gate. That's where the biggest pressure will come. Kyle will be in charge there.

The second group will patrol the northern perimeter. They will have the pleasure of seeing Eleanor fly directly over their heads. Grace the Dragon will help you there.

Farmer Goodfellow will lead the third group. You will patrol the forest behind the launch site. We can't afford a surprise attack there. Montmorency the second and Montmorency the third will be with you.

Finally, I will lead the fourth group which will be stationed in the middle of the Hill Top Barn area to mop up any Brasser Thugs who get through the perimeters. You guys at the perimeters are all tough, so I'm sure my group in the middle will have an easy time!

Puma Cats, please keep an eye on everything and report in quickly where you see problems.

It's going to be tough. It's going to be nasty. So, everyone remember: "STAND UP TO THE BULLIES AND SAVE OUR PLANET."

While Zac was briefing his volunteers inside the launch perimeter, Oligarch was giving orders to his hired thugs in a large field at the bottom of the valley below the launch site.

"Right, you bunch of layabouts" Oligarch yelled. "No more mess-ups!

Last time, I trusted you thugs to do the job and nothing happened! This time, you've got senior Brasser management to make sure we get results. We have to destroy the space launch they plan. I don't care how it's done, it's smash the spaceflight time!

The key is to get in through the gate. That's their weak point. Yours truly, that's me, Oligarch, will lead the assault on the gate. Hoops is my second in command. We'll take half of you thugs with us. The lovely Marilyn with a Fist – and what a fist that is- will attack from the lower side of the field and try and move up towards the launch pad. When they see the size of Marilyn's knuckle duster, those namby-pambies will run a mile!

Lady Wrestler will lead a party through the woods above the field. That will divert attention from the mayhem going on at the gate.

Remember, we need rubbish to make money, so make rubbish of the SuperHeroes!"

Kyle, at the entry gate, was the first to feel the pressure. The number of thugs in front of him went from just a few to well over fifty. The volunteers linked arms and kept bats and staves at the ready as the thugs pushed forward. The thugs hurled insults and ugly threats were shouted. Bricks were thrown and Kyle was glad he had ensured all his volunteers had helmets.

No thugs breached the gate and it looked as though the volunteers would hold the line. Then Dr Wetherby-Good and Akito arrived in a Land Rover. They had to get into the site to check the final preparations. So, Kyle and the volunteers had to clear a path at the gate without letting the thugs through. Led by Oligarch and Hoops, the thugs hammered on the top and sides of the Land Rover. They shook and bumped the vehicle until Dr Wetherby-Good thought she was going to be sick. At the height of the battle at the gate, Kyle found himself right up against Oligarch in a furious scrum.

"I know you, young fellow" growled Oligarch. "You look like a bloke who could use some money, a bit of dosh. Maybe even a nice huge bling-bling designer watch on your wrist. I hang out in a nice café in Farnham. Come and see me and we can have a nice talk. Better than hanging out with these nambies. You'll never get a huge bling-bling designer watch on your wrist from them!"

Just as Oligarch finished talking, the Land Rover pushed through. A half a dozen nimble thugs were able to follow the vehicle through before volunteers from Zac's team could close the gap at the gate. For a moment, it looked like the break-through thugs might get to the launch site itself and destroy the Green Man's work.

Grace the Dragon saw the problem and temporarily abandoned her post on the northern perimeter. She moved quickly and breathed her terrifying fire at the breakthrough thugs. If the thugs were nimble getting through the gate, they were even more nimble getting away from Grace. At warp speed, they sprinted down the hill, jumped walls and fences and joined Marilyn's group at the bottom of the hill.

The Land Rover was safely in and the boffins could survey the scene and check all was ready for lift off. What they saw was action everywhere they looked. What they felt was the combination of stress, fear, excitement and the determination to succeed. The tension mounted every minute. The Superheroes now had forty-five minutes left before they had to launch. The Brassers had exactly the same amount of time to prevent the SuperHeroes destroying their dream of wealth.

The middle of the launch site was dominated by the Green Man's magnificent long-bow. Its huge stave was mounted horizontally on two huge wooden pillars both well dug into the ground. The bow and the bow string were at maximum tension; the bow string was secured by two huge ropes. These ropes were secured to strong posts also well dug in behind where the Montmorencies had scraped away the land. Both these ropes had to be cut through at precisely the same time to unleash the power of the bow.

A slim runway made of ash bridged the gap between bow and string at the greatest point of distance. On the string end, a small sled was secured. The angle of launch had been checked again and again. It was exactly in line with the scientific requirements.

As Akito and Wetherby-Good approached the launch pad, Eleanor the Invisible was saying her farewells to Ariadne. Eleanor looked magnificent in her outfit, a true space warrior, poised and equipped for the greatest mission of her life.

"There is no doubt of your success. Your mission is a noble one," said Akito to Eleanor.

"Your courage is amazing, you are an inspiration to us all," said Wetherby-Good.

"You are a superstar," said Ariadne. "Fly well and return safe. And look after that incredible cape and suit. I need to borrow them when you return!" Ariadne and Eleanor embraced and then Eleanor turned to start climbing the short ladder which would allow her to get on to her launch sled.

Eleanor showed great calm and poise. It was a different story in the rest of the Hill Top Barn area.

The maximum pressure was at the gate where Oligarch and Hoops were demanding more and more from their thugs. It was not pretty.

"Forward you wastrels, kick these nambies out of the way! Trample them underfoot! Bury them!"

A huge scrum formed. The thugs threw small rocks and bottles. The volunteers suffered cuts and bruises. Exhaustion was becoming a real factor. It was only a matter of time before the thugs broke through. Kyle made his defending volunteers form a wall of bats and staffs and linked arms. He called for every reserve that Zac could let him have. He even asked for the Montmorencies whose weight and strength might make the difference. For the moment Zac would not agree, so Kyle had to hold the line with the volunteers he had. He knew it was only a matter of time. Could they hold out another fifteen minutes?

At the bottom of the slope, Marilyn was rallying her troops for repeated attacks. Her fist was repeatedly raised in the air as she led charge after terrifying charge. Eleanor from her perch on the launch sled could see the glint of the knuckleduster on the raised fist. For a moment, her calm was gone. She thought about what would happen if Marilyn's thugs got through. In truth, it was only continued dragon fire from Grace that prevented this. And Grace was running out of flame power.

In the woods behind the launch site, a different kind of game was being played. Lady Wrestler commanded a small group of thugs among the trees. She avoided any kind of full-frontal attack, and used her thugs to create diversions. A feint here, a rush there, immediate withdrawal if challenged by the volunteers skilfully led by Farmer Goodfellow. The only serious battle behind the launch site happened when Lady Wrestler led an attack on a huge pile of branches just on the edge of the woods. The branches were positioned carefully, almost as if they were hiding something. As soon as Lady Wrestler attacked, Farmer Goodfellow gathered all his forces including the Fjord horses and drove the thugs back.

With five minutes to go, it looked as if the SuperHeroes and their volunteers might be able to hold on. Eleanor was on her launch sled. The longbow was at full tension. Two woodsmen with sharp axes were poised by the retaining ropes to cut them through at the precise same time. Akito started the official countdown.

"Five minutes and counting," boomed across the Hill Top Barn launch area over the speaker system.

"Its now or never for our dosh!" screamed Oligarch to the thugs at the gate. Smash them, trample them. Forward!"

It was at four minutes to countdown that Zac got the call he had dreaded all morning.

"I can't hold on anymore!" screamed Kyle. "My volunteers are exhausted. The thugs are getting through the gate in large numbers!"

Just as he heard these words, Zac saw four thugs had burst through. They were rugby-tackled just short of the launch pad by members of his mop-up squad. His rugby-trained group could handle four thugs but not the hundreds that were about to surge through the gate and destroy the launch pad.

"Two minutes and counting," came the voice of Akito.

"Plan big M's!" Zac shouted over the speaker system.

The pile of branches in front of the woods began to move. A couple of individual branches fell and then a very large arm emerged. The pile moved even more and a dinosaur came out of the pile. The dinosaur turned immediately and started clearing more branches from the pile.

"Come on Montmorency the third," screamed Montmorency the second. "We've got work to do. Wake up, and get your lazy butt in gear. And I bet I can do much more damage to thugs than you can!"

Montmorency the third appeared, shook his huge head to wake himself up and started to work with his brother clearing all the remaining branches. They uncovered the huge pile of rocks they had removed during their dig on the launch site.

"Better hurry, my brother!" screamed Montmorency the third. "Otherwise there will be no rocks left and no more thugs to scare off."

Montmorency the third hurled the first rock. His accuracy was SuperHero class. The rock landed on Oligarch's left foot as he drove his thugs through the gate and into the launch area.

"Arghhhhhhhhhhhh!!" Oligarch's scream could be heard over the whole of the Surrey Hills.

The whole Hill Top Barn area fell silent. Then the second rock landed on the thugs in front of the gate. Then a third rock. Then a fourth rock. The effect on the thugs was devastating. The rocks brought with them bruises and cuts and bumps and broken bones and total terror.

The thugs at the gate didn't wait for the fifth rock. They fled. No amount of dosh could justify standing up to this barrage. They ran (or in the case of Oligarch and other of the wounded, hobbled) down the hill to get as far away as possible from rock-hurling dinosaurs. Marilyn the Fist's thugs witnessed everything that happened. They stopped their attacks when they saw the first rock fall. They didn't like the idea of rocks coming their way.

"Ninety seconds and counting" boomed Akito's voice.

The volunteers relaxed all across the launch site.

Relaxed volunteers were just what Lady Wrestler and her gang of nimble thugs were looking for. The removal of the large pile of branches had created a big gap in the defence lines. Lady Wrestler and four thugs were through it like lightening. They danced around Farmer Goodfellow and through the legs of the dinosaurs.

"Sixty seconds and counting."

"See the woodsmen with the axes?" shouted Lady Wrestler to her thugs. "I will throw one to the ground; you thugs seize his axe. The launch plan will be ruined!"

None of the mop-up gang could catch Lady Wrestler and her thugs. They moved at warp speed, weaving and dodging. They could see the longbow clearly. They could see the two woodsmen ready to sever the retaining ropes when the word was given.

"Fifteen seconds and counting. "

The woodsmen raised their axes. Lady Wrestler was poised to dive at one of the woodsmen and knock him over.

"Ten seconds and counting."

Lady Wrestler felt a juddering in the air behind her head. Then a whistling sound, ever louder. A large rock missed her head by a tiny margin and smashed into the ground halfway between her and the woodsman.

Lady Wrestler needed all her skill to dive over the rock. She landed in a crumpled heap, dazed and badly winded. All she could do was gaze dizzily up at the sled carrying the magnificent Eleanor.

"Five four three two one. Longbow lift-off!"

The woodsmen cut through both retaining ropes with absolute precision of timing.

The pent-up power of the longbow was released. Eleanor hurtled into the air with energy and speed beyond belief.

Oligarch hobbling painfully down the hill towards Clandon looked up and saw Eleanor in all her magnificence, flying like an arrow way over his head. The pain in his foot, the sight of Eleanor and perhaps more than anything else, the cheering and applause from the Hill Top Barn area, made him sick with anger.

"You may have won this time," he roared at Eleanor high above him. "But it ain't over yet. Not by a long shot. Now things are going to get really nasty for you do-gooders. You won't destroy my plan to make all my friends rich. I will destroy you!"

Back at Hill Top Barn, Claire was awarding three beautiful bouquets. The first two went to Montmorency the second and Montmorency the third. They were still arguing about who was the best digger and whose rock had halted Lady Wrestler.

The third bouquet went to a still dazed and confused Lady Wrestler herself. For the most spectacular and most amusing dive of the battle of Hill Top Barn!

CHAPTER NINE. ALONE IN SPACE.

"Terrifying, electrifying, exhilarating." Eleanor's memory of the longbow launch would stay with her for as long as she lived. Immediately the retaining ropes were cut, she felt immense pressure through her whole being. Without the magical space suit, she would have been destroyed by the vibrations and juddering as her sled accelerated across the short wooden runway.

Then, airborne, the ground dropping underneath her. The terror gradually replaced by a sense of calm. She could see the Brasser thugs fleeing the barrage of dinosaur-hurled rocks. Even at the speed she was travelling, she glimpsed Oligarch, flailing his fists in fury. It was almost as if Oligarch's anger was fuelling her flight.

In honesty, Eleanor was glad to be away from the Brassers and their fierce violence. She was now alone on a journey. She was in charge of her own destiny. She could not fail the planet. She passed over the towers of Woking looking down on the deep canyons between the buildings. Her speed increased as the boost of her new magic cape and gloves kicked in. She climbed through the thin cloud, and banked west to set the course for her orbit of the planet. She started to get a whole new view on the place she lived. For the first time in her life, Eleanor could view big sections of the Earth. The whole of Southeast England. Its soft green hills and compact towns and villages. Then, as she climbed higher, coastlines, rivers, the pattern of a whole continent lay beneath her.

She flew over the Atlantic Ocean. She crossed the North American continent, heading north west towards Alaska where it was still dark. The lights of towns and cities below her a beautiful mosaic. Over the Canadian border, she boosted the power of her cape and boots. Very soon, Eleanor would leave Earth's orbit and head out towards the Star from Afar. A call came in from the transmitter-receiver. It was Ariadne's voice.

"Time to go to maximum boost. Go, SuperHero lady! Fly to save the planet!"

Once Eleanor was sure she was on a clear path to the Star from Afar, she could look back on the beauty of the Blue Planet. She experienced an overview that changed for ever her perspective on life and the way we live it. Eleanor took in the whole planet in a single glimpse. It was beautiful beyond all belief. Beautiful beyond all possibility of improvement.

"If only," she said to the cosmos, "if only I could get the Oligarch up here to see this. Even he with all his power, all his aggression, all his lust for more would be overcome by the beauty of our Blue Planet.

A single glimpse would be all it took to convert him to caring for what we have in place of always seeking more. It's a great thought," she told the cosmos. "But I need to get real. It's not going to happen. Not in the next few days anyway!"

She knew now with absolute certainty that she must succeed in her mission. She could not allow the beauty she saw to be destroyed. Eleanor focused on the task in hand. She checked her direction and recalculated the timing. Everything was in good shape. She needed to rest. She needed to recover from the excitement of the launch. She needed to recharge her energy for the task ahead. Relaxing in space was easy. There was no sound. No people shouting. No cars or motorcycles. No radios, televisions or telephones. No arguing or fighting. Absolute quiet. Eleanor closed her eyes. She slept. She dreamed of savage thugs threatening her. She dreamed of being shot into the air like an arrow. She dreamed of stars and constellations, the Milky Way and far-off galaxies. She dreamed of moons and stars. She dreamed a lot about an amazing Blue Planet. She dreamed of returning to her SuperHero friends and working with them in the natural beauty of the Surrey Hills.

The alarm buzzer on the transmitter-receiver woke Eleanor with a start. Less than half a mile away, she was shocked by the bulk of the Star from Afar.

"Wake up, sleepy Eleanor." The voice on the transmitter-receiver was crackly, broken, but unmistakably Ariadne's. "Time to get ready to board the Star. If you don't get things moving now, you'll drift right on by. Then I'll never get to wear your marvellous costume."

The Star from Afar was exactly as Eleanor had seen through the telescope. But now it was real, immense, forbidding, grey and greasy. Scientists will tell you that you can't smell things in space. Astronauts will tell you differently. Eleanor would side with the astronauts. This Star stunk. The smell was old, stale and frightening. It almost made Eleanor sick. It was the smell of thousands of years of accumulated putrid rubbish. Eleanor forced herself to accept she would have to work in this smell. Better overcome it here than allow it to pollute our Blue Planet. Eleanor adjusted the power of her cape and boots. She had to navigate carefully to get close to the huge Star. She had one simple objective. Place the transmitter-receiver on the Star. Securely and in a place where it could read all incoming and outgoing messages. New messages and those that had been sent in the past.

Lights on the transmitter-receiver told her if the device was well placed. Red light meant it had no access to the messages. Green was positive. The light was red.

One of the wires which suspended the small object from the huge blimp-like object above was now right in front of Eleanor. She grabbed hold with one of her powerful gloves. Immediately she was spinning round the wire this way and then the other. Dizziness overcame Eleanor. The foul smell seemed to get worse. It was almost as if the giant rubbish Star was fighting against her. Pushing her away from its foul secret. She lost all sense of where she was. Ariadne's voice came over the transmitter receiver.

"You must stabilize yourself with your magical cape and gloves. Quickly. If your dizziness gets worse, you will spin off into space. All will be lost!"

It took huge effort fighting down the dizziness and getting power back through the cape and gloves.

"This daughter of a Surrey Hills woodcutter hasn't come all this way to drift dizzily in space," she told the cosmos.

At last, she was back in control. She looked at the lights on the transmitter-receiver. Red.

"So, what shall I do? Go down the wire to the small object or up the wire to the giant rubbish Star?" she asked the cosmos.

"I think small is beautiful," she said. She descended toward the small object.

The light shone brighter. But still red. Eleanor reversed direction and moved up along the wire to the huge rubbish Star. Light still red. The smell stronger and stronger, making Eleanor wretched to her stomach. She reached the top of the wire where it was anchored to the rubbish Star. The surface of the Star was grey, greasy. Without gloves, Eleanor would not have been able to bring herself to touch the foul Goldbeaters skin.

Light still red. Maybe a little less bright. For twenty long minutes, Eleanor navigated around the foul Star fighting the smell, fighting the sickness, resisting the huge urge of flying back to the Blue Planet. Then, in the distance, she saw an object sticking out of the Star. It was yellow. Something metal, mechanical. Eleanor navigated closer. The lights

flickered. Red, then green, then back to red. There was a familiar faint buzzing in Eleanor's head. "ZZZZZ…." It is what she heard when water was protecting her from danger. The water in her spacesuit was talking to her. Working with her. Protecting her from potential harm. She navigated closer to the object. It was the back end of a rubbish collection truck! Painted yellow. Now filthy with rubbish. Black, muddy wheels still attached. Back of the truck open.

"This is how the rubbish was loaded into the Star!" Eleanor told the cosmos.

Eleanor got closer and closer to the back of the truck. The foul smell was overpowering, sickening, the desire to escape from this awful place more and more difficult to resist, the buzzing in her head louder. Then the light turned a continuous steady green. Eleanor looked inside and towards the front of the truck. There, where the windscreen would normally be, was a giant control panel. Computer lights flashing. A hundred dials showing information. And most chilling of all, a huge television screen in the middle showing a picture. The picture was an aerial view of the

Surrey Hills! In front of the control panel sat two figures. They were adjusting wheels and levers on the control panel. Eleanor hadn't seen anything like these figures since she had watched the Tin Man in The Wizard of Oz. But were these figures living beings or were they robots?

The buzzing in Eleanor's head was intense. The light on the transmitter-receiver a bright green. She didn't wait around to find out whether living beings or robots were on the rubbish Star. The transmitter-receiver device was highly magnetic. She clamped it to the inside of the truck. She made one last check on the two figures at the front of the truck. They were busy adjusting levers. She didn't think she had been noticed.

Eleanor got out of the back of the truck. She hung on to the side. She no longer had the transmitter-receiver, so she had lost all contact with the Blue Planet. She was alone in space, clinging to the outside of a foul truck anchored to a huge object stuffed with rubbish. She took out the astrolabe that Ariadne had given her. That would be her saviour. She set a course for home and powered up her cape and gloves. As she moved away from the rubbish Star, the smell reduced. The buzzing in her head decreased and became softer, more relaxing. She became calmer, more composed in the knowledge that information from the transmitter-receiver was already reaching the Blue Planet.

Eleanor had only travelled one quarter of the distance home by the time all the information from the Rubbish star had reached Akito and Dr Wetherby-Good on the Blue Planet. Their enormous computer analysed the vast data bank in minutes. Now, everything was clear. The whole Star from Afar plan was plain to see.

Late on Thursday night, the Surrey SuperHeroes, minus their heroic Eleanor still in space, met for a full briefing. By the end of the meeting, everyone and especially the Green Man, knew exactly what they had to do. Very early on Friday morning, Akito and Dr Wetherby-Good gave a full review to the Powers that Be in London. On the basis of what they heard, at last the Powers agreed to act. Not as much as the SuperHeroes had asked for. Not by a long shot. But at least some support.

CHAPTER TEN. THE POWER OF BLING.

Later that Friday morning, at the very same library style café where Daksha had first come across the Brassers, Kyle was enjoying a very well-prepared cappuccino. To Kyle, it seemed the coffee was made even tastier by the fact that Oligarch had paid for it.

"Right, my good friend," said Oligarch as warmly as he was capable. "First things first. Let me introduce you to my colleagues here. You might recognize them from some of our other encounters. But since you are going to be practically one of the family, I'll do things formally. This here is Hoops." He gestured to the tall guy with a bandana. "This is the beautiful Marilyn with a Fist," whose hand Oligarch held to his lips in an exaggerated gesture. "At least she was beautiful until, like the rest of us, she got bumps and bruises and scratches. Wonder how that might have happened? Any ideas?

And sadly, the fourth member of our group, Lady Wrestler, can't be with us today. She had a nasty encounter with a big rock. Thrown at her by a horrible dinosaur. She's had to go to a nice hospital down in Cranleigh to recover. I'm sure you'll want to send her your best regards.

But enough of all the nice chit-chat. That doesn't make money. What have you got to tell us about the famous Star from Afar, and the activities of your namby-pamby friends, trying to stop decent people from making an honest living?"

Kyle looked at Hoops then Marilyn with a Fist then straight into Oligarch's eyes.

"As it stands, the only thing I can tell you is that the SuperHeroes know everything there is to know about the Star from Afar. They also have a plan to deal with it. And they are getting support from the Powers That Be."

"That's no bloomin good!" all warmth gone from Oligarch's voice. "We need details, boyo. Without details we can't stop the Superheroes wrecking this business opportunity. So, cough up!"

"For details, you are going to have to pay. Simple as that," said Kyle.

"I told you, cloth-ears", said Oligarch aggressively. "I'll give you a top of the line huge bling-bling designer watch. Even better than this one here that I'm wearing." Oligarch waved his watch in Kyle's face.

"That's nowhere near enough. What I can tell you will give you the opportunity to be incredibly rich. You can be the richest man in the world," said Kyle, with more confidence than he felt inside. "Without my info, you'll get nothing out of this whole Star from Afar business. So, I want my fair share of all the loot that the Brassers will make. If I tell you everything you need to know, I'm not going to be very popular around here. So, I need to look after myself."

"Cut through the blah, blah, blah, what do you want to spill the beans?" shouted Oligarch.

"First, said Kyle, "I want two huge bling-bling designer watches. One for me and one for my beautiful girlfriend. Then, I want cash, paid into my bank."

Kyle passed a piece of paper to Oligarch. There was a number written on it. A number with a lot of zeroes after it. Oligarch looked at it. Then laughed.

"You're off your rocker! I can't afford this. Out of the question."

"Oh yes, you can afford it, I checked up on you. This is only about half what your worth. It's no problem for you. If we can't agree on it right now, I'm not saying any more. Then you can kiss goodbye to making mega money on the Star from Afar." Kyle got up and started to leave.

"Calm down, boyo." Oligarch called out to Kyle's retreating back. "Don't get your underwear in a twist. You're getting a heck of a deal, but okay. I'm a nice bloke, so tell us what you know."

Kyle turned around and walked back. Again, he looked straight into Oligarch's eyes.

"First, I want to have the huge bling-bling designer watches on my wrist. Both of them.

Then, I want you to transfer the cash right now to my bank account. And give me proof of the transfer."

"Out of the question," replied Oligarch. "It will take time to do all that."

"Time," said Kyle, "is something neither you nor I have much of. So, I'm on my way." He turned to leave again.

"All right all right, tough guy," said Oligarch. Then he turned to Hoops and Marilyn. "You two, make sure pretty boy here doesn't go anywhere. I'll be back in fifteen minutes. And if he wants more coffee, make him pay for it himself."

He glanced at Kyle as he left the café. "It had better be good, what you tell me. For your sake!"

For fifteen minutes, Kyle, Hoops and Marilyn sat in stony silence. Kyle occupied himself checking out the impressive bumps and bruises on his companions' faces. Just as Kyle began to think that he was being double-crossed, the café door crashed open and Oligarch stormed in. He banged two elegant huge bling-bling designer watch cases on to the table in front of Kyle and then thrust a cash transfer slip into his hand. Oligarch put his face only a few inches away from Kyle's. "Right, let's have it, make it snappy and make it good!"

Kyle took the time to check the contents of the two huge bling-bling designer watch cases and then studied the cash transfer slip.

"Right," said Kyle. "Listen carefully. Despite all the Brasser efforts, the space launch was successful. A transmitter-receiver was securely placed on the Star from Afar. We have seen and analysed every piece of data received by and sent from the Star since the project started. The Star and the small object below it are both packed with rubbish. Rubbish accumulated over hundreds of years on a planet in another galaxy. The beings who live on the planet want rid of the rubbish. They want to dump it somewhere else in the universe. It's clear that the beings on the planet had big arguments before they sent the rubbish away. Some didn't care where the rubbish went. Others didn't want to dump it anywhere that caused problems to other living beings. They finally agreed that before the huge load of rubbish dumped, they would test out getting rid of a small amount. If there was no reaction to the small load of rubbish, then the huge load would go to the same place. So, we now know that the small load of rubbish will be sent down to Earth this weekend. If there is no reaction, they will simply assume this is a good place to dump rubbish. Then the much bigger load will follow.

We now know where and when the smaller load will land. The SuperHeroes have devised a very clever plan to show that the rubbish is not welcome on Earth. The Star from Afar will then move on." Kyle paused. Then made as if to get up.

"Not so fast, my fine fellow," said Oligarch. "You are going nowhere until we know exactly where and when the first load of rubbish will land and what the SuperHeroes plan to do about it."

"Oh yes, almost forgot that," said Kyle. "The rubbish will land in the Surrey Hills. More precisely, the so-called test drop will hit Bramley on the large green where the cricket field is. It will crash down to earth at huge speed at exactly midday this Sunday.

The SuperHeroes have devised a clever plan to bounce the rubbish, still in its space container, back into space. If the rubbish bounces back, that will be a signal that we don't want other people's rubbish here. If the rubbish doesn't bounce back, then a very large amount of rubbish will follow. The Green Man is devising a piece of apparatus that will bounce the first rubbish container. But I have no idea what it will look like or how it will operate. I do know the Green Man is very skilled and he'll construct something that will work. The Powers That Be know everything you know. They are closing all the roads in the Surrey Hills to motor traffic from midnight tonight. So, all you nice Brassers have to do is stop anything getting into or out of the Bramley cricket field area from now on. If the SuperHeroes can't get into the field, they won't be able to build their bounce machine. If the machine isn't there, the rubbish will simply crash into the Surrey Hills. And then very soon after, the whole of the Surrey Hills, in fact the whole of the planet, will be a rubbish tip.

Knowing the SuperHeroes, they will not be put off by the ban on motor traffic. They will try and bring in materials by horse and cart, maybe even by hand. Stop them and the test drop rubbish will land on Sunday. Then the rest will follow. The Brassers will get what they want. You will all be mega-rich. And I will be well out of here. So, good luck Brassers. You've messed up twice. Don't mess up a third time. And thanks for the coffee!"

With that, Kyle was out of the door and down the street away from the café, as if propelled by the Green Man's longbow.

Kyle's emotions were in turmoil as he ran towards the railway station. He had two magnificent huge bling-bling designer watch watches in his possession and a ton of money in his bank account. But would everything work? Would he ever be really safe?

– ■ –

As Kyle was agonising over what he had just done in the Farnham cafe, Eleanor was completing the final part of her epic space journey.

She was re- entering the atmosphere of the Blue Planet. This was a highly dangerous part of her journey, since if she got things wrong and descended too fast, her mission would end in a fiery ball. Fortunately, Eleanor was totally focused on navigating. She was blissfully unaware that virtually all the information she had worked so hard to get was now in the hands of her deadliest enemies, the Brassers! She had become expert in using the astrolabe given her by Ariadne. So, at exactly the right moments, by adjusting the power in her gloves and using her cape as a parachute, she was able to descend towards the Blue Planet without overheating. A marvellous sight greeted her when she was about a mile above her beloved Surrey Hills. There, flying above the green hillsides, deep forests, and sweet rivers and ponds, was Grace the Dragon. With great skill, Eleanor navigated a gentle landing on Grace's neck. From here Grace would fly her home.

For a few moments Eleanor enjoyed a sense of relief. Her journey in space, her terrifying experiences on the rubbish Star, her long journey home with no direct contact with the Blue Planet, all these challenges were successfully behind her. Eleanor was looking forward to a long rest. Then Grace the Dragon shattered the illusion.

"Well done, Eleanor," said Grace "You are a true SuperHero. But unfortunately, no peace or rest for you. I have to fly us to an urgent meeting with Dr Wetherby-Good and Akito. Be prepared for some sleepless nights!"

In reality, had Eleanor flown back into a whole new set of problems?

CHAPTER ELEVEN. BOUNCE RIGHT BACK.

Oligarch organised the Brassers thugs with skill and speed. To the dismay of the local inhabitants, the first of his thugs arrived at the Bramley Cricket ground late Friday afternoon. They found the big green space deserted. They did catch sight of several Puma Cats among the trees at the edges of the field. They shouted at them in very rude terms, telling them to go away and then hurled insults and empty bottles at them. It seemed the Cats vanished. But there again it seemed that some re-appeared during the evening and the night. You could never be sure what the Puma Cats were up to. Even the Brasser Thugs realised that.

Right up until midnight, more and more Brasser thugs arrived, by car, motorcycle and mini- bus. The roads in the Surrey Hills then closed but still the Brassers army arrived on foot or on bicycles or scooters. Under the orders of the Oligarch, Hoops, and Marilyn the Fist, they formed a human chain right around the field. The chain was ten, even fifteen people deep in places. Nothing, not even a Puma Cat, could sneak in. And there was absolutely no site of the Green Man or any of the other SuperHeroes.

At 4 o'clock on Saturday morning, the Brassers saw the first sign of SuperHero activity. A large farm cart pulled by two Fjord horses came down the road from Shalford. The cart was laden with wooden poles, ropes and great bundles of the Goldbeater's skin that had been used for Eleanor's spacesuit. The cart was being driven by Farmer Goodfellow and, next to him, sat one of the Rugby Club volunteers.

Hoops and a group of fierce looking thugs stopped the cart well before it got near to the Cricket field green.

"And what have we got here boys?" shouted Hoops in an aggressive tone. "What's all this about?"

Farmer Goodfellow was taken aback by Hoops' tough manner. He stumbled over his words a little.

"Oh, good morning, good morning gents," he said. "I, er… that is we, er…are not really sure what we have here. You see, we are er…, well we are just working for the Green Man. I suppose you know him………?"

"Get to the bloomin point, grandad!" interrupted Hoops. "What do you want here?"

"Well, we want to unload these things on the cart that the Green Man has given us. We need to unload them right in the middle of this green field. But all these people seem to be in the way. Perhaps you nice gentlemen would be kind enough to help us?"

"I will do you a big favour, grandad," replied Hoops. "Get yourselves and your smelly horses and your old cart out of here right now, before you get hurt!"

"But if we don't unload these things, the Green Man will be most upset. And he's very big and very strong, so we don't want to upset him, do we?"

"I couldn't care two figs about your Green Man. And you can tell him that from me. Now, I'm going to count slowly to ten. If I reach ten, and you haven't started to turn around and leave, I will ask these people here that you call "nice gentlemen" to assist you. But I should tell you that, if they do have to help, they are liable to break things. I hope you follow my meaning."

Farmer Goodfellow and his volunteer partner decided that were out-numbered and out-muscled. Downcast, they turned the cart around and headed back up the road. No more carts arrived that morning, although there were continued signs that the SuperHeroes desperately needed to get on the green field. A dozen times, individuals carrying poles or ropes, tried to gain entry. They were turned around and sent away with big doses of Brasser aggression. What made more impression on the Brassers was the site of Grace the Dragon. Three times she flew low over the field, every time giving a quick demonstration of her ability to breath fire. On her third flight, Oligarch saw two hooded figures riding on her neck. "Was one of those that Eleanor woman they had shot into space?" Oligarch wondered. "What are these namby-pamby SuperHeroes trying on now?" Each time Grace flew over, the thugs got nervous. So, three times, Oligarch got Hoops and Marilyn to pass the word around. "Don't worry. We are in control. Nothing to worry about from silly old Dragons."

And the truth of it was, the Brassers were in control at Bramley. Oligarch called Hoops and Marilyn together for a quick meeting.

"Look", he said, "it's way too early to celebrate but things are going our way. If the SuperHeroes are going to get some contraption built here, they are running out of time. They need it built by tomorrow morning and thanks to our efforts, they have made no progress. None at all. Every time they try to get on the field, we completely knock them back. Frankly, they are a pathetic namby-pamby lot. I tell you what I'm going to do. I'll give Lady Wrestler a call, see how's she's doing and share the good news. I'll put it on my speaker phone, so we can all hear." And with that, Oligarch called Lady Wrestler's number.

"Good Morning, my dear, this is your good friend Oligarch. How are you?"

"Well," came back Lady Wrestler's voice. "The Cranleigh Hospital has let me go. Nothing worse than a strained knee and a twisted ankle both of which are strapped up. But…..."

Before Lady Wrestler could go on, Oligarch cut in.

"That's great. Let me tell you the stuff I've been doing." Oligarch related the details of his meeting with Kyle and went on to describe everything that had happened at Bramley.

"So," he concluded, "I've got those SuperHeroes nicely bamboozled. The Green Man can't even get on to the test drop site let alone build his wonderful contraption. The first load of rubbish lands midday tomorrow. I've got them in a right pickle."

"Actually," Lady Wrestler at last jumped in. "Actually, It's you that are in a pickle. And you've got all of us in the pickle with you."

"What are you on about?" Oligarch replied. "I think you must have hit your head and got everything jumbled up!"

"The landing site isn't at Bramley. It's here at Cranleigh on the Green. The Green Man has already built his contraption. I'm looking at it right now. It's an enormous trampoline, anchored by huge elastic cords to massive wooden stakes. The stakes are driven into the ground. The trampoline surface is made from Goldbeater's skin. It's all one ginormous bounce machine. And the first rubbish doesn't land tomorrow. It lands right here in about an hour and a half. It's you that's got jumbled up. You've been bamboozled by Kyle. He's sold you the most expensive and useless bill of goods ever!"

There was a long silence. Then an ear piecing, agonising scream from Oligarch. Then: "I'm never beaten. I've still got ninety minutes. Hoops, Marilyn, get those useless lazy lump thugs down to Cranleigh at super top speed. We just need to make one big rip in the trampoline surface and the namby-pambies will be beaten."

"Oligarch, have some sense," chimed in Marilyn. "All the roads are closed. We'll never make it to Cranleigh in time."

"Get with the program, Marilyn! Use the old railway line that runs from Bramley to Cranleigh. Get the fittest five hundred thugs. Get them bikes or scooters or let them run. Tell them if they're not down here in less than sixty minutes, they'll be the ones bounced into space! Right, Lady Wrestler, you sign off now. Keep us posted and pitch in and help when we arrive. We'll be there in a jiffy."

Lady Wrestler cut the connection. She then turned to make the long tour around the trampoline. As she moved, she almost bumped into someone who had been standing close to her. A young girl, with beautiful long glossy hair. Lady Wrestler moved on. She had lots of spying out to do. She just hoped her conversation with Oligarch had not been overheard.

In fact, she had been overheard by Amy Elizabeth, who had been helping build the trampoline. She immediately relayed the news that the Brassers now knew about Kyle's deception. A plan was put in place.

Meantime in Bramley, Oligarch, Hoops and Marilyn were whipping the thugs into action. Hoops led all the fast sprinters and set off immediately. Oligarch and a group of thugs got hold of every bike in the area, using all their skills in begging, borrowing or stealing. He and Marilyn found a tandem and led the "Tour to Cranleigh" at top speed. The remaining thugs either grabbed scooters or walked or they stayed there, eating and drinking. Within fifteen minutes of the call to Lady Wrestler, nearly five hundred thugs were heading at speed to Cranleigh on the disused railway line. Their progress was remarkable. It's amazing what you can do when you have to. The charge was led by Hoops and his sprinters, then Oligarch and Marilyn on the tandem.

Oligarch took a look at his huge bling-bling designer watch. Only about twenty-five minutes before the test container of rubbish landed but they were only a half mile from Cranleigh. All they had to do was get off the disused line, get to the Green and make a big rip in the trampoline.

"Pedal faster and we'll be home and dry," shouted Oligarch to Marilyn, behind him on the tandem. The namby-pamby SuperHeroes will never beat me!"

At that moment, they saw the huge ditch right across the old railway line. Oligarch screeched to a halt. The ditch was deep and wide, way too wide to jump across. There was loads of stinking mud at the bottom. Impossible to slide down one side and clamber up the other. The ditch completely blocked the place where they had to get off the old railway line and reach the big green at Cranleigh. Oligarch stopped. The sprinters stopped. All the sprinters and runners stopped and the riders all backed up behind them. They were jammed.

Marilyn noticed a sign on the other side of the ditch. It read "Welcome to Dinosaur Gulch!" She pointed it out to Oligarch.

"I'm not going to be beaten by a couple of stupid dinosaurs!" Oligarch screamed. He turned to Hoops. "There's a big building supply warehouse just back on the line. Take a bunch of your thugs and get enough wooden planks to cross this stupid ditch. And hurry, hurry, hurry!"

Hoops and his team rushed off, and within ten minutes were back with a load of strong, wooden planks. The bridge building could start and the nearly five hundred waiting thugs could start to move again. There was still time for the Brasser army to reach the Green and rip a huge hole in the trampoline. The rubbish would arrive and the massive load would follow. They would earn the huge rewards they dreamed of.

Meanwhile, on Cranleigh Green, an emergency meeting was taking place between Amy Elizabeth, a Puma Cat, Grace the Dragon, Eleanor, Vesta and Kyle.

"The Brasserrrs were stopped by the ditch which the Montmorrrencies dug. But they have found a way to build a brrridge." said the Puma Cat. "They will soon be here. Then big trrrouble."

"It is still ten minutes before the rubbish drop hits," said Kyle. "They can still wreck everything. We have to go to Plan X."

"If we have to, we have to," said Vesta." But I must tell you all that both Eleanor and I are exhausted. The plan will take huge energy. We will both be testing our powers like we have never tested them before. But what has to be, has to be."

With that, Eleanor, Vesta and Kyle climbed up on to Grace's neck. They pulled hoods over their heads. They prepared for the most important flight of their lives.

Back at the disused line, the bridge had been secured. Oligarch and Marilyn were preparing to cross on the tandem. The stalled army of thugs behind could now move on to the Green, damage the trampoline and win the day for the Brassers. It was at this moment that they saw Grace the Dragon rise in the air above the trees in front of them. Three hooded figures were mounted on her neck. The sight was terrifying, awe inspiring. The whole thug army stopped their advance.

The first figure on Grace's neck pulled back his hood. It was Kyle. He had a megaphone, and addressed the Brasser army.

"You have one last chance to retreat and disappear back to your homes. If anyone crosses the bridge, it will be disaster for all of you. You have been beaten at every turn by the SuperHeroes. Go back to your homes."

"Don't listen to him," shouted Oligarch. "He's a liar and a cheat. Follow me and we'll all get rich!"

At this, Oligarch and Marilyn started to ride their tandem across the bridge, screaming at the thugs to follow. As the thug army began to move, Eleanor threw back her hood and stood up on Grace's back. Eleanor had extraordinary powers with water. Water protected her when she was in danger. All Eleanor's powers in the past had been in connection with rivers, ponds, lakes and pools. She had never before tried to use her powers as she used them now. She was exhausted from her long space flight and the task ahead of her was immense. Eleanor looked up at the sky above and opened her arms wide. She called for a gigantic rain storm in the Surrey Hills, right over Cranleigh.

Immediately, huge black clouds darkened the sky. Powerful lightning bolts with enormous claps of thunder. Then the rain. Immense rods of water pounding down. Flash floods on the old railway line. The whole thug army drenched to the skin in moments.

The storm disappeared as quickly as it had arrived. But its power had halted all movement in the thug army. They stood immobile. Drenched and in awe of the power of nature.

"Come on you wastrels," screamed Oligarch. "It's just a little shower. Have none of you got wet before? You've nothing to worry about. Look at that silly Eleanor lady. She's totally exhausted. You've nothing more to fear from her. She'll disappear in a moment just like always. Come on with me. Still time to get rich!"

At that, Oligarch surged forward again, dragging Hoops and his team of thugs with him.

The third figure on Grace's neck stood and threw back her hood. It was Vesta, Goddess of Fire. She too was tired. Exhausted from work over thousands of years. Her great skill was the creation of fire KAPOW, and the freezing of fire KAPOW- KAPOW.

She had never before tried to freeze water. But summoning all her energy and pointing both hands at the drenched thug army, that is what she did.

KAPOW- KAPOW- KAPOW. All five hundred thugs on the path were imprisoned in frozen shirts and frozen jackets and frozen hats and frozen shoes. They were all frozen to the ground. They were frozen stiff. Not one of them could move.

Still hanging on to Grace's neck, Kyle looked down on the frozen thug army. He saw Oligarch at the front, frozen on his tandem. He looked into Oligarch's eyes. Kyle knew that Oligarch was beaten. Kyle, Grace and even Vesta and Eleanor exhausted as they were allowed themselves a brief moment of triumph.

Then a rushing of wind, which quickly became a roaring in their ears. A huge WHOOSH- WHOOSH- WHOOSH wiped out all other sound. The container of rubbish from the Star from Afar was about to hit the Surrey Hills. It was close to smashing into the huge trampoline that the SuperHeroes had built on Cranleigh Green. This would be the trampoline's ultimate test. The sound of the container of rubbish hitting the Goldbeater's skin surface of the Green Man's trampoline was so loud, so deafening, so frightening, so awe inspiring, that people gave it a special name. A name that was remembered for a long, long time. It was called "The monster clap that echoed all around the Surrey Hills."

The weight and enormous speed of the capsule immediately sank deep into the surface of the trampoline. It sunk lower, lower, lower, right into the big hole the Dinosaurs had dug out below the trampoline. The elastic cords stretched and screamed. The huge wooden posts bent inward. It looked as if the whole trampoline would buckle and collapse under the enormous strain.

But the Green Man and his team of magicians and forest workers had done their job well. At the critical point when the rubbish container was at its deepest, the strength of the trampoline was at its maximum. At this point, the container stopped pushing at the trampoline. The trampoline started unleashing its awesome energy against the container. The acceleration was unbelievable. The container rocketed upwards. It left the surface of the trampoline at huge speed. It powered into the air and surged away from the Earth as if fired by a thousand rockets. Within minutes, the container was out of the Earth's atmosphere and back into space.

CHAPTER TWELVE. IMPORTANT ANNOUNCEMENTS.

On Saturday evening just as people were finishing their supper, the Powers That Be released the following Important announcement.

"We are pleased to tell you all that the object known as the Star from Afar is now moving away from our planet. This follows an action plan put in place by the Powers which included shutting all the roads in the Surrey Hills. You are all safe. No significant damage happened in the Surrey Hills. You can now go back to your normal lives.

The work of the Powers has prevented a vast amount of rubbish being dumped on our amazing planet. Rubbish that would have destroyed the beauty of the Surrey Hills and polluted the whole planet. This is a timely reminder to us all to care for the beauty of the place we live. Do not spoil the planet by polluting it with waste. Be responsible in everything that you do.

The Powers That Be would like to thank all who helped ensure that their action plan worked. This includes a small group of Surrey Hills locals under the leadership of two Professors from the Science Centre.

– ■ –

On Sunday morning, Akito and Weatherby- Good picked up this message from the transmitter on the Star from Afar. "We are moving our space vehicle away from the Blue Planet and setting our course for a long journey home. We have seen that dumping our rubbish on the Blue Planet is not what those who live there want. We want to apologize to all living things on the planet and indeed to the Blue Planet itself, for even thinking of this.

We have learned much over the last few days. You cannot dump the rubbish and pollution you make on others. You have to deal with it yourself, or even better, stop making it. In future, we will place all our energies behind this and stop sending rubbish somewhere else.

We would like to thank the group on the Blue Planet who helped us see the stupidity of our actions. In particular, we want to recognize the incredible bravery of the lady who flew into space and placed the transmitter-receiver on our space vehicle. We hope this lady has safely returned to her beautiful home. Both our pilots were particularly taken by her gorgeous cape, space suit and helmet. They send their love."

A week later, Vantage Point a magazine local to the Surrey area reported the following news item:

"Surrey ambulance and rescue crews saved the lives of nearly five hundred walkers and cyclists last weekend. They were caught in a major downpour in the Cranleigh area. With the current cold weather, they all nearly froze to death. All those rescued were charged by the police for causing a disturbance and failing to keep the peace. They were all later released on their commitment that for the next five years, they would use all their efforts to help preserve the beauty of the Surrey Hills."

The magazine also reported that a Surrey Hills multi-millionaire who simply went under the name of Kyle had made a huge donation to a Surrey Hills charity whose aim is to keep the area productive and beautiful. Apparently, Kyle had made his money by buying and selling huge bling-bling designer watches.

Part of the money was being used to establish a fitness and training gym, to be run by the well-known personality, Lady Wrestler. All lessons and training in this gym would be free.

REAL LIFE SUPERHEROES

GEMMA – A caring nature.

Gemma's claim to Surrey Hills SuperHero status can be summed up in two words. "I care."

Gemma radiates care. For her family and for everyone she meets. She goes about her work with immense care. She cares about the environment from her Surrey Hills home. She cares about the future of Planet Earth.

Perhaps the most striking thing about Gemma's caring attitude is that she has sustained it through really tough challenges. Challenges that might have knocked many of us off course. Far from knocking Gemma off course, the challenges simply brought out the Surrey Hills SuperHero in her.

Today, Gemma's lifestyle defines "success." She and her husband have a wonderful family, including a gorgeous recently arrived granddaughter. Gemma runs her own company which is, not surprisingly, in the "caring for skin" business. Gemma is a much-respected professional among the group of local Surrey Hills entrepreneurs and artisans.

From the outside, it looks like Gemma has arrived at a perfect destination. The journey, however, has been a roller-coaster.

Gemma was born in the UK but really grew up in the United States. Her parents split up when she was in her formative years and that created its own challenges. Gemma stayed with her mum and came back to England where she studied for an Environmental Studies degree. Gemma may not have realised it at the time but it's this science background that gave her the skills to formulate her own skin care products.

Gemma met James, her future husband in GAP. They weren't shopping together for t-shirts and jeans. Gemma was working for much needed cash and James was her boss! James quickly saw Gemma's caring nature and ability to relate to the customers and gave her the "front of house" role. Gemma and James stayed in touch and eventually married. They have a family of three wonderful boys. This is the "all boy band" Gemma wants to work together eventually in her skin care business Puremess.

If you ask Gemma about the determination she shows in her business activity, this is what she tells you: "I would say that I always had the energy and the drive to succeed. The focus? I think that came as a result of my fight with cancer. It's no fun fighting off cancer three times. I have the scars, they are part of my life. I asked my husband once, "Do the scars bother you?" He said, "As long as you are on this planet, everything is fine" So I thought, well, if I'm going to stay on the planet, I need to create a new me. Make good informed decisions and have clear goals that shape my legacy.

That's where the skin care product idea came from. When you fight cancer, you have to think about everything that touches your body. And then I thought, 'Why wouldn't everyone want to think like that?'

I started to formulate 100% natural skin products. I began making them in my garden shed. I took them to farmers' markets, specialty stores, and then offered them online. People liked them. They liked the natural ingredients. They liked the fact that everything can be recycled.

The business is growing. We have a small team. We're not yet big enough to employ the whole family but customers keep coming back for more. So, watch this space."

Gemma's message is clear. "Find something you care about, and keep going no matter what life throws at you."

That's what Surrey Hills SuperHeroes are all about.

MARK. Changing people's lives for the better

Mark is a man of action. You see it as soon as you meet him. In addition to his job as an IT consultant, he's always got a project going on. He's accomplished a lot. He's crazy about rugby and coaches Mini Rugby for Guildfordians RFC on Stoke Park. He's a fanatical member of the Guildfordians walking rugby group. He became involved with Scouting through his son and has contributed significantly to the Scout Explorers, Beavers, Cubs and Scouts for many years.

Mark's qualities are easy to spot. He is determined, energetic and curious, always interested to learn. He is inclusive in everything he does. He is modest about his achievements, always giving credit to others for what the team has accomplished.

There are many stories that can be told about Mark. This one focuses on a tragic event that threw a huge roadblock in Mark's path. It caused him to stop, reflect and breathe deeply before moving forward. The story involves two groups of people in very different parts of the planet who together go through life changing experiences. One group in Kathmandu in Nepal. The other, the Scout Explorer groups in Guildford, Merrow, Ripley, Cranleigh and Shalford/Wonersh (known as the Surrey Hills unit). We'll start with Kathmandu in Nepal.

It's early in the second millennium and Scouts worldwide are looking forward to celebrating the centenary of the Scouting movement in 2007. One of the Surrey Scouting leaders, Hilary Byrne, is working in Nepal. She is stunned by the incredible beauty of the area. She is shocked by the lack of basic facilities such as running water on-site in Nepalese villages and the impact this has on Nepalese families who have to walk long distances to reach a fresh water spring or a single standpipe.

Back in the UK, Bernard Pentecost, a legendary Scout and larger than life character, is thinking about ways of celebrating the centenary of the Scouting movement in 2007. He meets Hilary who is in the UK on a trip home. Together, they formulate a plan of three elements. A working element: helping people, who have so much less than we do in Surrey to get a basic fresh water supply. A cultural element: understanding the values and customs of people living in very different circumstances. A tough trekking element: a hike to Everest base camp.

The project gains momentum and, in the Surrey Hills, Mark finds himself involved. Surprise, surprise, he feels the project is a perfect fit for his energy and outlook on life. He throws himself into it. He puts together a party of twenty Scout Explorers from Guildford, Merrow and Ripley. He knows that they have to raise significant funds for the materials they will need to get the fresh water from the standpipe to the individual homes. The group take a fundraising stall on Ripley Farmers Market. They sell tea, coffee and cakes. Gingerbread Men baked at Mark's home become a massive favourite at Ripley. The plan is coming together. The team is gelling. The finances are building. The departure date is not far off.

Then suddenly, unexpectedly, tragically, in late 2006, Mark's wife died. Through the grief of his loss, Mark is still determined that the trip should go ahead although he doesn't really believe that he will be able to go. He does know that more funds are needed, so he takes on the job of baking Gingerbread Men. As to going to Nepal, Mark has massive doubts. The pull of helping people gain a fresh water supply is strong. But Mark has three young children to think about and the family has to handle the grief.

Friends and relatives step in. They persuade Mark that there will be two huge benefits if he goes to Nepal. The trip will be a key factor in helping him deal with the grief. And it will help the village school get a supply of fresh water. It's a win-win. Mark goes. The family care for the two younger children and Chris, the eldest at fifteen, joins the group going to Nepal.

The trip proved to be an amazing physical and cultural learning experience. From the start, everyone in the group was taken outside their comfort zone. The work started at a small very basic school outside Kathmandu. Hard digging was involved to connect the school to a large fresh water pipe about half a kilometre away. Kids from different backgrounds formed the Surrey team. Everyone had to learn to work together and bond as a team. The reward for their tough labour came when they saw how their work changed the lives of people who had previously had to haul their water long distances.

The experience changed the attitudes of the Surrey group. The Nepalese were very poor and had very few possessions. But they smiled a lot and were relaxed and calm. The Surrey group quickly began to see that people didn't need material things to be happy. In fact, they realised material things can make you unhappy!

When the water supply project was completed, the group went back to Kathmandu where their organised trek to Everest base camp would start. If the digging was tough, the hiking was a whole other challenge. The group all discovered that, however tough they thought they were, the Nepalese porters and Sherpas were tougher. The reward for all the hard trekking was sunrise over Everest on Easter Sunday.

The group returned to the UK as stronger, wiser people. Mark returned with his beliefs reinforced, ready to accept the challenges of his new situation.

There was also an unexpected bonus. The trekking company which had supported the Surrey Scouts on their trek to Everest turned out to be a bit unusual. This company helped communities across the country and asked the Surrey Scouts if they would come back to run water projects in some of their mountain villages. Bernard and the team seized the opportunity and ran a further four trips with the last in 2015, returning from Nepal just weeks before the catastrophic earthquake.

This account was written with massive input from Mark, the Surrey Hills SuperHero of this story. He stuck at it through difficult personal times. He helped keep the team together when many were out of their comfort zones. He saw another culture, admired the way they lived and took great strength from it.

Mark sees it a bit differently. He sees all the Scouts involved as SuperHeroes. They all worked hard and survived as a team through tough times. He sees the Nepalese people as SuperHeroes – always doing tough jobs for little reward, always happy and smiling through adversity.

You can decide who you think the SuperHeroes are. But maybe it doesn't matter. Maybe the lesson here is that, inside every one of us there is a hero who can do extraordinary things. One sure way of finding that hero is go to the Surrey Hills, admire the natural beauty, see what nature and man in harmony can do and breathe deeply. You may be surprised by what happens.

MARIANNE. Following a dream and bringing great music to the Surrey Hills.

In 1989, well beyond the memory of many readers, a film called Field of Dreams was released. It starred heartthrob of the era Kevin Costner. It told the story of a farmer in Iowa, USA who is passionate about baseball. He dreams that if he builds a baseball stadium in the middle of an Iowa cornfield, people will flock to see the games. His farming neighbours think he is crazy. This is farmland, not the city. So few people around. But his dream tells him that, if he builds the stadium, people will come. He builds the stadium – and the crowds arrive. It's a good movie, worth viewing.

So, I'm sure a question is already in your mind. "What has a thirty-year-old movie about an American sport and set in the USA got to do with music in the Surrey Hills?"

The link is this. Follow your passion with determination and professionalism and good things will happen.

174

This is the story of Marianne who runs and plays in a hugely successful Jazz Club in Guildford. She brings great music to the people of the Surrey Hills.

Marianne's story is not straightforward. She didn't always plan to be a Jazz musician or the owner of a Jazz Club.

In fact, Marianne studied Classical music at school and learned the cello. After school, she went to Surrey University to study physics and software engineering. She lost interest in music for a while. Then, for the social contact, she played electric bass for a band who performed pop and rock favourites for parties and pub evenings. She got to know the singer in the band who persuaded Marianne to go to a Jazz workshop. This is the tipping point. Marianne falls in love with the Jazz but is baffled by the technique. She sees it this way, "Classical music is all about getting it right, Jazz is all about hearing it right." Marianne buys a double bass and works and works at becoming a Jazz musician.

On the business and professional front, the story is more complex. Marianne's professional career is going very well and she is on the board of a local Company. The prospect of her running the Company is there. But the music is calling. By 2010 she is asking herself a key question. "Do I progress in business which provides a good income? Or do I follow my passion and start a Jazz Club where the word is that you can become a millionaire but only if you start with two million?" After a lot of agonising, Marianne decides to follow her passion.

She starts performances at a pub in Farnham where the landlord has an interest in Jazz. Marianne runs Jazz workshops and undertakes one-on-one teaching. She gains huge satisfaction from helping others on their Jazz journey. Jazz Club performances move to the Electric Theatre and then to Guildford Rugby club. Marianne attracts major Jazz talent from London and beyond and audience numbers build. Then lockdown hits. Marianne gets around it by doing "livestream" performances out of the Boiler Room. Once lockdown lifts, the Jazz Club attracts sell-out audiences at Guildford Cricket Club. Outdoor venues in the Hills are back on the agenda, with Wood Street village and Loseley big favourites.

So, what drove Marianne to make the life changing jump from a well-paying business career to starting up a Jazz Club? There are lots of elements in the mix. Marianne's determination to progress her playing skills on the double bass is a key one. Through the Club, she now plays with and learns from top musicians. She also loves the ambiance of Jazz, its cross-cultural nature, its inclusiveness. She wants to get more women into Jazz, still a male-dominated music form. She works to get young people into Jazz. She started and is Chair of the Cheryl King Trust. This provides financial support for young people to learn a musical instrument who might not otherwise have the funds to do it. A significant number of young people across Surrey are being helped by this charity.

In short, Marianne followed her passion and made the jump. She saw the challenges of the music and the values it stood for and realised that the Jazz world was for her. Standing up for values and rising to challenges is second nature to Surrey Hills SuperHeroes.

One thing is for sure: thanks to Marianne, you no longer need to leave the Surrey Hills to enjoy world class Jazz.

MAKE YOUR OWN SURREY HILLS SUPERHERO STORY.

Writing and illustrating your own Surrey SuperHero story can be great fun. You can let your imagination run wild! All you need is some drawing paper, a pencil or pen and some crayons. Just follow the simple steps below. You can create your own SuperHero story on your own or with friends and family.

IF YOU MADE UP A STORY ABOUT A SURREY HILLS SUPERHERO – WHO MIGHT IT BE?

WOULD IT BE A PERSON – OR AN ANIMAL- OR A "MAGICAL PERSON?"

WOULD IT HAVE A SPECIAL NAME?

WOULD YOUR SUPERHERO LIVE ON HIS OR HER OWN OR BE PART OF A FAMILY OR GROUP (LIKE THE DINOSAUR BROTHERS).

WHERE WOULD YOUR SUPERHERO LIVE? In a Surrey Hills town – or in the Hills- or on a farm?

HOW WOULD THEY DRESS? Would it be modern dress or old-fashioned clothes – or something totally imaginary and magic?

WHAT WOULD THEY DO IN THE SURREY HILLS?

WHAT WOULD YOUR SUPERHERO LIKE TO EAT?

COULD YOUR SUPERHERO RUN QUICKLY OR SWIM OR FLY?

WOULD YOUR SUPERHERO BE VERY STRONG – OR HAVE SPECIAL MAGICAL POWERS?

WHICH OF THE OTHER SURREY HILLS SUPERHEROES WOULD THEY BE FRIENDS WITH? The Dinosaurs? Eleanor? Vesta? The Green Man?

WHO MIGHT THEIR ENEMIES BE? The Brassers? The red-faced man with the smelly car? The people who throw litter in the forest?

HOW WOULD THEY BECOME SUPERHEROES OF THE SURREY HILLS? Write a short story about their adventures.

WHAT WOULD THEY LOOK LIKE?

- SKETCH THEIR FACE

- SKETCH THEIR ARMS AND LEGS

- SKETCH THEIR BODY

- WHAT CLOTHES WOULD THEY WEAR?

- PUT IN A BACKGROUND OF THE SURREY HILLS

If you feel really good about your SuperHero story, you can send it to the author (Steve) at the following email address. You can take photos of your illustrations and attach them to your mail: -

Stevemarkwell1l@gmail.com

Steve and Cathy will be excited to read your stories and will send you back any comments they have.

The illustrations below were done by Steve's grandchildren, Cam, Matt, and Fred. They made them after they first listened to the stories. We hope they also inspire you.

Cam aged 13

Matt aged 11

Fred aged 6